The Blinks

'Shy'

by Andrea Chatten

Illustrations by Rachel Pesterfield

First published in 2017 by

The Solopreneur Publishing Company Ltd

Shortwall Court, Pontefract, West Yorkshire

www.thesolopreneur.co.uk

ISBN 978-0-9934527-0-3

Printed in the U.K.

For further copies, and other titles in the series, please go to - www.oodlebooks.com. Also available on Amazon and Kindle.

To Andrea

"Thanks for all
your love & support"

Much love

Andrea Chatten xxx

CONTENTS

Dedication

This book is dedicated to Jacquie, Paul and Bryan, the best in-laws anyone could have.

Chapter 1

Nazim

This is Nazim.

Even if you went to the same school as

Nazim you probably wouldn't know who he was, as Nazim fades into the background wherever he is. Don't get me wrong he's not invisible, but that is how Nazim feels most of the time.

Nazim has always been very, very shy. Even when he was little and attended playgroups where all the other children were laughing and having fun, Nazim was usually clinging to his mum's side crippled with fear. He much preferred to be with Mum as she let him stay there and hide, although it was quite different when Dad was there.

Dad found Nazim's shyness frustrating. He too had been shy as a child and remembers how many situations he missed out on through fear of what lay ahead. Dad told many stories of children's parties he never attended, experiences he missed out on and friendships he never developed. Dad didn't want this for Nazim; he was determined for his son to have more.

However, this meant that Dad got it wrong with Nazim a lot of the time. In parks and playgrounds, Dad would drag him over to children he didn't know, introduce him and ask the other children if Nazim could play! Poor Nazim felt so nervous in those situations that sometimes he found he couldn't even speak!

Other times, Dad would push Nazim forward to make sure he took part in exciting events. Once, when they were on holiday, a petting zoo was the special attraction at the local village fayre. Looking at the animals from a distance was fine for Nazim, in fact, he surprised himself when he came out from behind Mum and showed a genuine interest in the tarantula.

Nazim didn't like spiders at all. The speed of them and the thought of them wasn't something he liked, but this one seemed almost too big to be scared of. She almost looked like a magical character from another world. Her lovely furry body and gentle nature made him feel less fearful. Never would he ever have thought about touching her, but a closer look was definitely something he wanted to do.

"Do you like the tarantula, Nazim?" asked Dad, noticing Nazim's new found interest.

Nazim didn't reply in situations like this as he always seemed to say the wrong thing, which led to things happening which he rarely liked.

"Come on! Let's get closer, maybe you could hold it?"

Nazim grabbed Mum but Dad's enthusiasm was stronger than his grip. Before he knew it Dad was introducing himself to the animal assistant. Nazim felt sick. You see, sometimes he felt like he was in a different time zone to everyone else, always wanting to do things slower than his world allowed. Dad's world was most definitely a rollercoaster (not that he had ever been on one)!

Nazim then felt the other familiar feeling that he has a lot, like he is dreaming. Suddenly the present moment disappeared and Nazim felt as if he were somewhere else and looking down. This happens because his mind is flooded with very strong emotion and fear that it causes him to drift away from what is happening in the present moment.

It is those moments that scare Nazim the most because when you are not in the moment, you can't protect yourself from possible threats or dangers which feed the imagined or real fear even more.

Nazim watched on as Dad held the tarantula in front of him. He just stared. He knew Dad was trying to help him but he really didn't want to be there. With what happened next, he wished he had done what Dad wanted.

Dad brought Dotty the tarantula closer towards him. Nazim wanted to flee more than ever. As he turned his head to look for Mum, he was met with hundreds of unfamiliar faces. Some were smiling, some were laughing, some were straining to see if the little boy would touch the huge spider. Where was Mum?

Nazim suddenly felt like he was the entertainment and his only talents were shyness and fear. He began to panic; he needed to get away from all the eyes on him. He saw a space between the crowd, in the direction that Mum had been. Then his worst nightmare happened.

As he turned quickly to bolt, his arm reared up and knocked Dad's hand, the hand with Dotty the tarantula in! The crowd gasped. Nazim froze. Dotty flew up into the air! She seemed to be flying in the air for ages. Everyone looked up in amazement. Eventually Dotty started dropping to the ground but thankfully landed on the head of the owl which made it look like he was wearing a wig!

Laughter erupted in the audience,

followed by clapping and cheers. This truly was Nazim's worst thing imaginable. He needed to get away from there as quickly as possible.

As he bumbled through the endless crowd, people patted him, said well done, rubbed his head - all the things that showed attention that he didn't want. It seemed to take an eternity to find Mum but eventually, there she was with a baffled-looking Dad and a sneering older brother and sister.

This wasn't the situation that developed Nazim's deep shyness in front of people, as that had always been there, but it certainly didn't help. It probably made him more anxious and fearful of people in general, especially crowds.

Nazim couldn't ever remember feeling happy in front of people. He wasn't too bad in front of his family, though his brother and sister always seemed to find something to pick on him about, so that didn't help him. Nazim's lack of confidence caused him to struggle every day in social situations.

Here are a few of the things that Nazim hated about his shyness...

1. Most people thought he was rude or unfriendly.

2. The smallest things upset him or hurt his feelings.

3. He always felt like his shyness label was a bad thing.

4. He compared himself to other people all the time and came off worse.

5. He was told all the time to look people in the eye but found this very difficult.

6. He didn't like who he was so tried to hide it.

7. Getting things wrong in front of people terrified him.

8. He wasn't good at anything, but

that was because he never tried in case he failed.

9.   He always felt like he was a failure and let people down.

10. He rarely enjoyed new experiences so felt like he missed out a lot of the time.

From the list, hopefully you can now imagine how difficult it was for him most of the time to live a human life, being around people all the time and feeling like Nazim felt. The demands of the day were huge.

Although Nazim attended school every day, it usually took so much out of him to try and be who he thought he should be. Everything was hard. His shyness seemed to be his enemy. It made him suffer when answering his name in the register, sitting with people on his table and moving from classroom to classroom. Being in the dinner hall and eating in front of others was particularly tough and walking in or out of assemblies made Nazim feel like everyone was looking at him.

Break times were the most difficult. He rarely had anyone to play with as he was seen to be boring. He didn't say much or do much and so tended to just blend in with the scenery, which is where he usually was. There were a few other shy children in the class - Sophie, Bailey and Juwairyyah (pronounced Ju-vair-ee-a) but Nazim was even too shy for them so they eventually gave up trying to be his friend.

Nazim had learned that being quiet protected him from lots of difficult situations. When he was younger, he tried for a while to be more confident but it all went wrong.

Once he was with some of his classmates and he was so pleased to be with them that he was desperately trying to think of something to say. What he hadn't realised was the conversation had turned to pets they had all had in the past and how sad it was when they had died.

Poor Halleemah had just wiped away her tears after recalling how she still missed Sniffy and Crusty, her beloved guinea pigs.

All the group started showing kindness and sympathy to Halleemah. Everyone, that is, apart from Nazim who had been trying so hard not to be shy that his brain was unable to listen to any of what was going on at the same time.

While everything had been happening around him, Nazim had thought of something to say and had found the courage to say it. Without delay, he asked the group what the silliest joke they had heard was.

This didn't go down well. The group departed and left Nazim stood on his own, uncertain about what had just happened. Nazim was devastated and very embarrassed. It was also made worse by the fact that they all told on him and he was told off by his teacher, Mrs Waters. Nazim decided that being confident wasn't for him so from that day forward he decided that he would stay safe and say as little as possible. But as you can imagine, this decision brought many more problems along the way!

Chapter 2

Meltdown

Most mornings, Nazim woke up feeling positive. It was only when he remembered about what his day could be like, that his mood shifted. This was partly because in the safety of his own sleep, he had the chance to be all the things he wished he could be.

At night, Nazim was funny. He could say things that would make the whole class laugh. He once had a dream that he and Mrs Waters were a double act and as she said something funny, he came back with something funnier. Having the power to see all your classmates happy and you were responsible for making it happen, felt like a dream come true.

Sometimes in slumberland, Nazim was confident. He was able to do jobs for his teacher, or he could answer a question in the assembly, or he could ask one of his classmates round for tea.

Not all of his dreams needed to be so spectacular. Some of the best feelings were when he woke up and just felt normal. Normal was all Nazim wanted to be. A normal person, who could have normal friends and could live a normal life, free from what he felt was the shyness curse.

Sadly for Nazim, his superpowers only existed during the hours of darkness. The reality of his day was not something he wanted. His day was scary; he lived in fear of someone asking something of him and him not knowing what to do. It was lonely being locked inside himself, unable to play outside. He once had a dream he was a tortoise and that was quite close to the truth, as that was where he hid most of the time - inside his human shell.

Nevertheless, Nazim lived day to day without anyone realising the reality of just how difficult it was for him. Children just thought he was dull and didn't want to be their friend. His teacher knew he was shy so didn't push him and his parents just coped with the fallout every night when he came home.

Most nights when Nazim came home, he was so tired from just being, that he ended up collapsing from the demands of the day. This usually meant he got cross at the smallest thing or sobbed and sobbed out of mental and emotional exhaustion.

Mr and Mrs Alam had had this almost every day since Nazim started junior school. Infant school had been okayish. The first few months of reception were hard and Mum had gone home feeling sad at leaving him most mornings, but school always said he had settled and enjoyed his day.

Nazim remembers infant school very differently. His teacher was always cross and he seemed to make her cross very easily. He felt he had no choice to do the things he needed to do. Being told off in public wasn't an option. He also got whisked along by other children in the class who left him no choice but to play with them. Sometimes he liked that but as he got older, people stopped trying with him and he became more and more withdrawn.

Every parents' evening, his mum and dad were reminded how shy he was and how difficult it was for him to talk with people. Once in a very busy art lesson, Nazim felt so ill that he went under the table, emptied his pencil case, was sick in it, fastened it up and kept it under his jumper until home time. This was all due to his fear of speaking to someone.

When he got home that night, he didn't even tell Mum or Dad. It was only when his older brother Wazidul stood on the bulging pencil case that his cover was blown. This is what worried Mum and Dad the most. Nazim was so shy he couldn't even ask for help. Although they tried to give him their attention, it always seemed to be rejected so they left it thinking they were making things worse.

This was what also led to Nazim feeling very lonely. He never told anyone how he felt so no-one ever gave him what he needed. It was just him and his shyness forever and that was how it was going to be.

This had a huge impact on Nazim and

how he felt about school. Nazim hated his shyness and he hated how it made him feel. It was beginning to cause a bigger problem at home too.

The older Nazim got, the harder it became to adapt to the people around him. Other children were developing social skills along the way but Nazim had been a slave to his shyness for so long he didn't know how to be like them at all. His day was spent on an imaginative stage, in the role of someone who had a major part but had never been given his lines!

It was this enormous pressure that Nazim put on himself that led to his emotional outbursts at home. This was the only way that he could communicate all the difficult feelings he had inside him. Usually within minutes of being inside the front door, he would either go up to his room and escape into the computer fantasy world where he could be big and strong and powerful, or start crying at the simplest request.

Earlier that evening, Mum simply asked him what he wanted on his sandwiches the next day and he collapsed on the floor in a heap, wailing and hitting the ground in frustration.

As Nazim lay there in his bedroom later that night, he thought how home was the only place that he felt he could be honest and the only place he felt safe enough to express what he felt. Even though he knew he was constantly being judged by Wazidul and his sister Rukkiah, he felt at least he had Mum and Dad on his side, although he had started to worry that they too were going to get sick of him eventually.

Poor Nazim didn't know what he was feeling and he certainly didn't know what to do. That night, Mum knocked on his bedroom door and asked if she could talk with him. Nazim invited her in.

"Have you had a tough day, Nazim? Do you want to talk about it?" asked Mum gently.

Nazim didn't know what to say. He knew in his head that a lot was going on, but he had no idea how to get it from his brain to his mouth.

"Is something the matter at school? Are people being unkind to you?"

Nazim felt he could answer that one. He knew no-one was being unkind to him, the problem was no-one was being anything with him because he wasn't being anything with them. "No," he replied.

"Who is your best friend at school, Nazim?"

This question wasn't easy to answer at all. How could he tell his mum he didn't have any friends? The fear of showing he was embarrassed combined with feeling tongue-tied left him not saying anything at all.

"I think I need to come and speak with Mrs Waters. You come home from school so unhappy. Something must be wrong."

Nazim felt sick. This was the last thing he wanted, even more feelings of embarrassment from everyone knowing how weak and pathetic he and his shyness really were.

Just at that moment, Dad came in. "Right Nazim, what is all this about? Your mother and I aren't going to put up with this rudeness and bad behaviour any longer. Now get downstairs and spend some time with your family."

Mum threw Dad a look of anger at what he had just said, but it was too late.

Nazim began throwing things around his room, screaming and crying at the same time. As Mum and Dad dodged the flying objects, Nazim felt like the worst person in the world. He could hear distant voices of Mum trying to calm him down, and Dad telling him off. None of it could be understood - his fear was now in charge and there was no stopping it.

Mum and Dad left the room but sat

outside the door, listening to things bang and crash. Eventually the room fell silent and Nazim slumped on the bed ashamed and exhausted.

Just as Mum was about to enter, Mr Alam spoke. "What are you doing? None of that behaviour was acceptable. I will not have a son of mine behaving like that. Nazim you are in serious trouble and we need to talk...urgently."

Mrs Alam didn't want to take sides and she knew something needed to be done. Her gut feeling though, was that her son was hurting, more than being naughty out of choice.

"I just need a minute with him, we will be down in a second. I am worried about him and shouting at him won't change what he is doing. You go and put the kettle on, we won't be long."

Mr Alam tutted as he stomped down the stairs and Mrs Alam went in to find Nazim curled up on his tear-soaked duvet.

"What are we going to do Nazim? What are we going to do?"

Chapter 3

Silence is golden

Throughout the night and the many nights that followed, Nazim tossed and turned, believing that he wasn't good enough.
He let people down all the time, which was obvious to him by how Mum had felt earlier.

Not even his dreams offered him comfort that night. He dreamt he found himself in a park surrounded by people, but knew none of them. Everyone was laughing, having fun and enjoying themselves. Nazim was alone. He shouted for his family several times but no-one heard or even noticed he was there. The dream ended with him becoming rooted in the ground while his body grew leaves and bark to camouflage him even more.

This dream summed up perfectly how unimportant he thought he was and how little he thought he had to contribute.

It also showed his constant fear of saying the wrong thing or of others being critical of what he did say. He also felt that he didn't have enough about him to compete with other, more confident people. Others were loud, bright and colourful in presence. This felt like a race that grey Nazim could never win.

Being shy was rubbish, he thought. Why him?

As he went downstairs for breakfast, his big sister Rukkiah tutted. "Mum and Dad argued all night because of you and your shouting and because I asked them to stop, I lost my phone for a full day. That is so not fair and it's all your fault. Just keep out of my way today. If I had a remote control for you, I would press mute and leave it like that forever!"

So she would mute him, would she? Well Nazim thought, her wish was his command. If it was what he'd said that caused all the problems, then not saying anything could ease all of that.

He pressed an imaginary button on his chest and that was the job done. Nothing was going to come out of his mouth today, not a squeak. Suddenly he felt excited and in control. Could he do it? That was the question.

He went into the kitchen. Rukkiah shot him a dirty look but that wasn't anything new. Wazidul didn't look at him at all. Mum smiled and said "morning".

Nazim smiled too and sat at the table

helping himself to cereal. Nothing was particularly different to a normal day... yet! Usual chatter was happening around him. Rukkiah and Wazidul were arguing. Mum was asking them to be more respectful to each other. Nazim looked on.

Then Mum started talking to him. "How are you feeling today Nazim?"

Nazim shrugged.

"Your Dad and I feel that something is wrong. I think it is because you feel unhappy, am I right?"

Nazim said nothing.

"I know this is difficult but we will get it sorted as best we can. Just tell us when you are ready."

Nazim thought that went quite well. It was easier than he thought, though he did feel bad for Mum as she was trying to help him. Phase one complete. Let's see how phase two will go - school.

Mum sent Wazidul and Rukkiah out of

the house early to school, as their arguing was starting to make her feel cross. Her attention then fell to Nazim.

"Okay Naz, let's get your things together for school. Do you need anything different than usual today?"

Nazim said nothing.

"Is your PE kit still at school?"

Not a word came from Nazim's lips.

"Nazim can you hear me?"

Nazim looked in her direction to register he could, but his lips remained closed.

"Right come on, shoes on otherwise we will be late."

Nazim showed he had listened and quickly put on his coat and shoes.

"Here is your bag, Nazim. If you don't need anything else, let's go."

Nazim walked out of the door and waited for Mum. She slipped her arm around his shoulder and pulled him towards her with a big squeeze.

"Do you want to talk yet?"

I am sure you can imagine what happened next. Yes, Nazim said nothing.

The walk to school stayed just like that, Mum trying to make conversation and Nazim keeping quiet.

Mum kissed Nazim goodbye and he kissed her back. As he walked in to school Mum felt more fearful than ever for her youngest son.

Nazim walked into school starting to feel that this could prove harder than he thought. Not answering Mum was tough but he had made a deal with himself to see if this could be the answer he needed. Strangely, this morning so far had made him feel bigger and more present than ever before.

The classroom was in the normal pre-register chaos with people changing reading books, the teacher's desk surrounded with children handing in homework and the rest of the class getting things out of their drawers ready for the day ahead.

Nazim headed towards his seat and remembered it was their weekly spelling test this morning. His heart sank. He hadn't even looked at them, never mind learned them. His stomach then flipped once more. On spelling test days, people were asked at random to read out how they had spelt a word, to see if they had it right or wrong. Then you had to read out your score.

Suddenly a wave of relief washed over Nazim. His new-found avoidance of talking would save him from both those things! He felt free. He was saved. Sadly Nazim had no idea about the reality of him refusing to talk, but he would soon find out.

Mrs Waters shushed the class. Everyone apart from Seth and Jemma did as they were asked. This was not unusual. Seth and Jemma always pushed things a bit further than was needed and always demanded the most attention they could from any situation. These two could be described as the opposite of Nazim. They oozed confidence, loved the spotlight and felt energised when all of the attention was on them. It was like they came alive.

Mrs Waters made a joke about them being their usual double act and the whole class laughed, which caused Seth and Jemma to be quiet for a while. Nazim looked on as he usually did, thinking that was what we all needed to be happy and feel successful in life.

The register was now being taken and Nazim realised it was getting closer and closer to his name. Suddenly a panic hit. By not answering the register he would draw oodles of attention towards himself which was the reverse of what this was all about.

Mrs Waters continued. "Max."

"Yes, Mrs Waters."

"Toyla."

"Here, Mrs Waters."

"Bobby."

"Bonjour, Madame Waters."

"Christopher."

"Hola, Senorita Waters."

"Why thank you, Christopher. You have made me feel very young today. Just so that you know for the future, a *senorita* is a young unmarried lady in Spanish. Everyone say 'senorita'. I am *Senora* Waters because I am a married lady. Everyone say 'senora'. If I was a man I would be *senor*. Everyone say 'senor'."

Nazim obviously resisted the early morning Spanish vocabulary lesson, but could he do the next part.

"Nazim."

Nazim looked in the direction of his

teacher. His teacher looked in his direction too.

"Nazim?"

Nazim froze. This was the hardest so far. To answer wouldn't be too difficult, as he had done this twice a day every day for the last five and a half years. The class all started twitching in their seats and turned to look at him.

"Nazim!" shouted Mrs Waters.

Nazim looked sad and startled, so Mrs Waters marked him present. His classmates started laughing and making comments about Nazim's lips being glued together. Bobby, who was sitting next to him, asked if he was okay and told the other children to pack it in and stop being so mean. Max sat opposite and started pulling faces at anyone who looked in their direction to try and get them all to stop what they were doing.

A half smile was all that Nazim could do to say thank you. He wasn't sure if he had made the right choice with this. How could he explain why he hadn't answered? This made him realise that remaining silent was now becoming the only option. Suddenly Nazim felt like he was stuck in quicksand and his decision to stay mute could lead to further danger.

He looked at the clock. It was 9.13am. The morning felt like it had lasted hours so far. Talking was a doddle compared to this. Today was going to be one very long day, that is if he could get through the spelling test!

Chapter 4

Any attention is better than no attention, right? WRONG!

After registration, the class lined up in a well-trained line for assembly.

Nazim went to his usual spot between Sophie and Amanda. He looked down as he usually did, to avoid eye contact with people just in case they saw in his eyes the nervousness he felt.

"It's okay Nazim, you don't need to explain anything to me," said Sophie gently. "I have days like that too where I feel overcome with my shyness and the fear of being around people seems greater than ever. It will pass, mine usually does."

Nazim's eyes widened, though he never

lifted them from the floor. Sophie had got it totally spot on. He never thought anyone else could feel like this.

Amanda turned around and agreed. "My worry and anxiety still gets me on some days but like Sophie said, I know it will pass and there are things I can do to make it feel better. Do you have things to try and change it on difficult days?"

Although he didn't know whether it was going to work or not, currently avoiding the things that made him feel awkward was the only tool he had, so he was sticking with it. He kept his head dropped and trudged towards the school hall.

The shyness always felt worse as he was queueing to go in to the assembly. His mind would become flooded with negative thoughts. Things like:

- o   What if I trip over?

- o   What if I fall?

- o   What if people think I am ugly?

- o What if people think I look scruffy today?

- o What are people thinking when they look at me?

- o What if others can see my shyness?

Nazim started breathing fast, too fast. The speed of his breathing meant he was taking in very little oxygen so his body began to panic. Sophie could see from Nazim's shoulders that something was wrong. She placed her hands gently on them to try and calm him but this made Nazim jump even more and he ran from the line towards the disabled toilets. Once inside, he collapsed on the floor trembling with fear.

Moments later, Mrs Waters could be heard on the other side of the toilet door. "Nazim it's me, Mrs Waters. Are you okay?"

At that moment, not only was Nazim so totally dumb struck that trying to breath was hard enough, he couldn't reply because of the pact he had made with himself.

"Nazim, I need to know you are okay. Can I come in please?"

Mr Quaile, the caretaker, had been summoned to the toilets urgently. "How is the little lad?" he asked gently.

"I don't know, he won't answer me," replied Mrs Waters.

"Hi Nazim, we need to know you are safe

in there and because you're not saying anything, I am going to have to take the door off. You don't need to be scared but there will be some noise," explained Mr Quaile.

The door lock was removed in what felt like seconds and as the door opened, Nazim gripped onto his legs terrified of what might happen next. Mrs Waters couldn't hold back her frustration. "What is this all about Nazim? You are behaving very strangely today. If you had just answered me none of this would have been necessary."

"Whoa! Be gentle on the kid. Look at him, he is trembling," said Mr Quaile. "It's okay lad, no harm done. Sounds like something has got to you today but I am sure it can all be sorted. Give yourself a few minutes and then you can have some time with your lovely, kind, UNDERSTANDING teacher, Mrs Waters."

Mrs Waters blushed, recognising how she had not been so understanding with him earlier. She moved towards Nazim and perched on the floor beside him. "Come on Nazim, the class will be out soon. Let's get over to the classroom and see what we can do to make this better."

Nazim was still shaking but managed to get himself to his feet. Mrs Waters walked beside him. They both looked pale and upset at what had just happened.

Mrs Waters looked at the clock. They had 12 minutes until the rest of the class arrived. What could she do to move this on as quickly as possible?

So far today Nazim had not said a word and so asking questions was pointless. She picked up his water bottle and placed it by the side of him. "Maybe a drink of water might help?"

Nazim was grateful for that. He took several gulps but then flushed with embarrassment when some drops fell from his mouth as he finished. He hung his head in shame.

"You don't need to be embarrassed in front of me, Nazim. I spent all Saturday night at a party and it was only when I got home that I realised I had a huge piece of lettuce covering my front tooth and no-one had told me! The only thing to do was laugh, or otherwise I may have cried!"

Nazim usually did cry.

"Anyway, it seems like today is proving a difficult day. We all have them, you know. I have lots."

Nazim was surprised at this. He thought grown-ups were all sorted. He knew she was a bit more shouty on some days but never before had he thought that maybe that was when she was having a bad day too.

"You remind me a lot of my younger brother, Nazim. When he was a bit younger than you, he developed a stammer. Do you know what that is?"

Nazim gave the slightest of nods. He felt a need to communicate somehow, as he wanted to hear this story.

"His brain is so sensitive, caring and intelligent that it mattered a lot to him what he said and how he said it. Not like me who just rambles on and on! He would get so overwhelmed with emotion mixed in with a bit of nervousness when talking in front of people, that his brain used to get a bit jumbled up and he would begin to stammer."

Nazim recognised those feelings. He had them a lot. Nazim looked in Mrs Waters' direction but didn't feel safe enough to look her in the eye just yet.

"Anyway, Keenan began to be bullied for his stammer. His classmates called him the meanest names until he too, like you, stopped talking. It went on a long time, way longer than it needed too. But for Keenan, not talking kept him safe and stopped him feeling so scared. Do you feel like that Nazim?"

Inside Nazim was shouting 'yes I do', but

sadly the words never came to anything and stayed locked inside.

"Keenan is 39 now. He still stammers now and then but only when he is tired or a bit stressed. It doesn't matter so much to him anymore. He is surrounded by people who love him and who know he is an amazing artist. You see, Keenan began painting and drawing when he stopped talking and he is now quite famous in the art world."

Nazim couldn't believe that something good could come out of something so bad. It could never happen to him though. He would always be boring, dull Nazim – the boy who had nothing to say.

"Oh, here are the rest of the class. If anyone is unkind to you today Nazim, you let me know. I won't have people bullying you like they bullied my little brother. We will continue this chat soon, I promise."

Nazim smiled a quarter smile. He had enjoyed that time with Mrs Waters. He felt alive. He felt connected. However, now was the time to hide away in his protective shell so that no-one could hurt him.

The class bounded in and took their seats quickly. Sophie passed Nazim and said quietly, "You okay?"

Nazim dropped his head feeling ashamed.

Jemma bounded over and said "Hey Naz, nice work being rescued from the toilet. Did they have to kick the door in? Ha ha, what a joke."

"Jemma Maw! Sit down and be quiet for once in your life. Sometimes it would be good for you, and a few others in here, to show some kindness towards other people and that everything is not one big joke to be laughed at," said Mrs Waters.

Jemma went to her seat where Seth high-fived her for a job well done in getting everyone's attention.

Nazim wasn't sure how today was going

to turn out. It was 10.02am and he was even more exhausted than on a normal day. He wasn't sure if he could do this on his own. He felt so alone. He was also beginning to worry as the choice of not speaking seemed to be weakening. Something felt like it was taking over and he was becoming physically unable to talk.

However, for those of you who have read any of these books before, you will know that children who are having a difficult time don't need to feel alone for too long, do they?

Chapter 5

Colin Confidence

Phew, thought Blink 24399 Colin Confidence as he sat up on the top of the striplight in Nazim's classroom. This child needs help and he needs it quick.

Colin Confidence had actually been watching Seth for a while. He would definitely benefit from understanding how his over-confidence affected other people. However, Nazim became the focus yesterday when it was noticed how badly his shyness was affecting him. The events of today had truly sealed it for Colin Confidence. Nazim was to become his next project.

The hardest thing for any Blink is reaching that decision. As Colin

Confidence scanned the classroom below, he noticed several children who could all benefit from a little bit of Blink help, as growing up can hard for all children at times.

He noticed Adam, who felt under lots of pressure all of the time because of what he thought he needed to be. Being okay wasn't good enough for him. He had very clever older sisters and was expected to be just like them.

The thing that Colin Confidence noticed about Adam was that he was easily one of the cleverest in the class but because of the added effort he pushed himself to, this made learning unenjoyable. It stopped him being able to focus.

Aneesha was another. She struggled every day with the thought that she was different from everyone in her class. She felt she didn't fit. She felt awkward, a bit like Nazim. She hated loud noises, so sitting next to Taha made the day seem very long and quite painful at times.

Abdul couldn't sit still. His energy exploded within him on many occasions and his motor just wouldn't stop. This caused many problems at home and school, as his brain didn't always kick in and get him to stop before he did something he usually later regretted. This hugely affected his sleep, as he had never learned how to turn his motor off and relax, so he usually laid there for many hours fidgeting and over-thinking.

Ellie thought she was ugly every day. She hated her face, her smile, her nose and her freckles, she most definitely hated the freckles. Many times Ellie would wish she was beautiful, a model that people gasped at when they saw her. She wanted to be prettier and had even started wearing some make-up for school, which she really didn't need.

Some of the children in her class thought Ellie was cool because of this, but little did they realise that the make-up was a prettier painting that Ellie brushed onto what she thought was her own ugly canvas.

Sid always thought he was fat. This thought was with him most of the time and so food was all he thought about. He tried to stop himself from eating sometimes in order to lose weight. This got him in a tangle which then made him so hungry that he would spend several days eating everything in sight and then feel so sick and horrible that he would not eat for days again. You can imagine how difficult this was for him and his family. His mum and dad had been worried sick but luckily Sid had started working with a lovely man who was helping him change how he felt about himself and food.

This list could have gone on and on because as you can see, we are all different in very special ways which is what makes us who we are. If Colin Confidence had the time, he could easily have shared it with every child to nudge some difficult situation forward, but that isn't always the answer.

However, Colin Confidence felt that all these children were beginning to realise how they felt and were starting to talk to people about it. This is one of the most important stages in changing things for the better as you will find out in the next chapter. He hoped they would start making positive changes soon and if they didn't, well then Colin Confidence knew where they were!

Colin Confidence had worked with children many times, helping them understand that growing up is about taking responsibility for yourself and your life, using those special people around you who are in your team and on your side. These people are your champions but if you don't use them, you'll never find out how wonderful their support can be.

It is also good to remember here that none of us really know what is going on in someone else's head, or how hard some days can be for others, or why some people don't always seem to make the right choices. This thought is at the heart of what the Blinks do. How many naughty or bad children do you think the Blinks have worked with? The answer is none. Zero. Nada! Zilch!!

This answer might surprise you but a huge part of being a Blink is to try and help other people understand this. Colin Confidence had spent many an hour explaining this to children, parents and teachers.

He remembers one child he worked with, Jake. Yes, Jake had done and still did quite a few 'bad' things, although Colin Confidence began by helping him understand that these were 'wrong choices' not 'bad' behaviours. Jake recognised this very quickly and was hugely relieved when he began to understand it. Yet the sadness he felt about himself wasn't so quick to change, as others reminded him of it every day. The problem was Nanna.

Jake lived with his nanna because he had been too much for his mum to handle. Sadly Nanna also found Jake difficult and believed he was a bad boy. This affected how she treated him. She had no patience with him, she felt he was having all his tantrums just to annoy her.

This made the situation with Jake worse. He never felt anyone understood or really cared to see things from his point of view. This made him feel more upset, angry and most of the time like he didn't care either.

Colin Confidence worked more with Nanna than he did with Jake on that project but when Nanna eventually grasped it, it was like a new universe had been created for them both. Their world became lit with sunshine and colour, even on greyer days and in the city of Sheffoold, there could be plenty of days like that!

The world began to feel warm again. It started to echo sounds of kindness. It smelt of love and hope. Things were getting better and better - they were getting there as a team and not as enemies. The most amazing thing was that Jake's bad behaviours reduced no end.

Don't get me wrong, he still made wrong choices now and then. We all do that though and if we learn from them, then hopefully we won't make the same mistakes again, meaning we have learned a valuable lesson in life.

Colin Confidence sat up from the comfy position he had found himself in, swaying gently on the warm fluorescent striplight and letting his mind wander. The children underneath him were busy tidying away ready for lunch. He looked for Nazim which was like playing 'Where's Wally?' in the group of children below. Where was he?

Very carefully, he tiptoed from the light to a bookshelf near where Nazim usually sat. His seat was empty. Colin Confidence looked towards the trays. He wasn't there. He headed into the cloakroom.

How long Nazim had been there was anyone's guess. His face was wet with tears, his cheeks flushed with shame. Colin Confidence wanted to introduce himself there and then so things could get going straight away. He couldn't bear Nazim feeling like this for a second longer.

Starting and finishing projects was the part Colin Confidence always found the hardest. It was something he needed to discuss at the midnight meeting later. He needed the Blinks' understanding as they were only too aware that the challenge at this time was where to start, how to begin and more importantly, when to meet!

Chapter 6

Magic at midnight

Colin Confidence stayed with Nazim all day. It was hard watching him have such a difficult day. The tears earlier had been because one of the children sitting on his table had noticed Nazim's quietness that day. Ned had stared at him across the table, then made his fingers into imaginary scissors and pretended to cut off his tongue. Although most of the class laughed, Sophie thought it was unkind what Ned did and so she told him so.

This led Mrs Waters to telling Sophie off for talking when she shouldn't have been and Nazim wasn't able to stick up for her when she had done something good for him. This had been the final straw for Nazim. He couldn't keep his feelings in any longer and so while everyone began tidying away, he ran for cover behind his coat in the cloakroom.

Although nothing worse happened across the day, the energy that was needed not to talk was very difficult and as the day went on, he got more and more tired. I am sure you can imagine what happened when he got home. It all erupted into one of Nazim's biggest ever meltdowns.

Nazim cried for hours and if anyone tried to help him, he got really cross at them for invading his most shameful feelings and so pushed them away, with some force. Luckily, the day ended quicker than normal with him collapsing into sleep just after eight o'clock.

As Nazim slept, Colin Confidence made notes about what the issues were and what he felt he could do to make this situation better. The Blinks were always a great help in any situation but it was expected that you thought for yourself first rather than expecting others to do the thinking for you.

Before Colin Confidence knew it, it was 45 minutes to midnight and so he needed to get a move on if he wanted to be there in good time. The journey there was always a pleasure. The calm of the night was peppered with movement below and all blanketed with a black, glittery sky. If you looked carefully up into the sky and amongst the twinkles, you would also see lots of movement too.

As you might already know, the hour before midnight is when all the Blinks in every city, town or village across the world move to a specially chosen meeting place for important Blink action. One thing these meetings all have in common is that it's the special place where local breads and sweet treats are produced.

Here are some of the ways to say bakery across the world:

Language	Word for Bakery
Albanian	furrë
Bosnian	pekara
Bulgarian	фурна
Croatian	pekara
Czech	pekárna
Danish	bageri
Dutch	bakkerij
Finnish	leipomo
French	boulangerie
German	bäckerei
Greek	Φούρνος
Hungarian	péksé
Icelandic	bakarí
Irish	bácála

Italian	panificio
Latvian	maiznīca
Lithuanian	kepykla
Macedonian	пекарница
Maltese	furnara
Norwegian	bakeri
Polish	piekarnia
Portuguese	padaria
Romanian	brutărie
Russian	пекарня
Serbian	пекара
Slovak	pekáreň
Slovenian	pekarna
Spanish	panadería
Swedish	bageri
Ukrainian	хлібозавод
Welsh	pobi
Yiddish	בעקעריי

So whether it's a boulangerie in France or a furrë in Albania, the chances are a group of excited Blinks would be meeting there at exactly midnight!

For Colin Confidence, arriving at the bakery made him feel like he was home. The familiar sound of Blinks' chatter. The sweet smell lingering in the air from the day's creations. The bakery made everything seem okay.

As usual the meeting was opened by Chief Blink. "Good evening wonderful Blinks. Let's spend a moment celebrating all the hard work we have done over the last 24 hours. Hurray for kindness, caring and the brilliant children out there who show real courage every day!"

The Blinks cheered with happiness. Colin Confidence smiled at his neighbouring Blinks.

"Let's not waste any time, there's lots to do. Blinks, please head to where you need to be. Have fun," said Chief Blink. The room became alive with motivation.

Colin Confidence jumped up and hot-footed it to the chocolate éclair trays where he met his friend, Blink 31271 Flynn Fabulous. "I am so excited about this meeting tonight as I have a child who I feel is perfect, but if am honest I am a little scared as the child doesn't speak at the moment and I don't have much understanding of that issue," whispered Colin Confidence.

"Me neither, but I am sure that the Wise Ones will be able to help just like they always do. Come on, let's get a good spot so we can start talking about it straight away," suggested Flynn Fabulous.

Some of the other Blinks were also scattering in organised chaos to where they needed to be too. Although they are all different in their own ways, they have similar elements between them which make them part of the same Blinks' club.

They also all have a number which shows how long they have been around. The smaller the number, the older they are. They also have differing shades of purple-iness through to orange-iness which highlights their individual levels of wisdom.

Some Blinks like to dress like humans and some in a unique Blink style.

Whatever they look like or however long they have been around, the place that they will always be at midnight is inside a bakery, in the city where they live. This is where all Blinks recharge their wonderfulness and experience the five phases of Blinkery!

Stage 1...*On the lookout!* This is the stage when the Blinks are looking for children who might need a helpful friend. They could either be in the research stage trying to find the right child, or have just found a young person who they feel might be ready for their help.

The chocolate éclair trays are in the main display cabinet and this is where all Stage 1 Blinks meet, new children are discussed and projects begin.

Any Blink who hasn't found the right child to work with yet helps create the sugar dough buffet. This involves snaffling any sweet crumbs or treats that are lurking in the bakery after cleaning.

This divine feast is shared by all Blinks at the end of the night and helps them boost their energy to get through the day ahead. It is also a chance to catch up with Blinks from far and wide.

Stage 2...*A good start.* Here the Blinks are happily working with a child and everything is going well. These Blinks learn from each other's past experiences and use them to think about what they can do next.

Stage 2 occurs on the vanilla slice board, which is also in the main display cabinet, but further back than the éclair tray. This tends to be the quietest stage of Blinkery as problems are a natural part of moving a situation forward, so when Blinks are at this stage it is all about celebrating good progress.

Stage 3...*Help!* This is by far the most popular stage, as most projects present challenges which need support. This stage meet on the large wooden bread shelves which cover the huge back wall of the bakery.

It is here that the Wise Ones are always on hand to share examples and stories of past projects so that valuable learning never stops. The Blinks know that it is very important to listen here so as not to miss any gems of knowledge.

Stage 4...*Eye spy.* When a project has finished and the child has worked hard to move things forward and change things for the better, the Blinks meet here. This happens on the fairy cake trays that sit in the window, and always feels very exciting as it is carried out under large white sheets of kitchen paper!

All Blinks would probably say that this is one of the best stages. At this stage, the Blinks feel that they get paid in fabulous feelings of satisfaction, pride, success and goodness. However, the real feelings of satisfaction only begin after the monitoring phase has happened as this ensures that the child involved has acted upon the two Blink rules:

✓ Each child involved in Blink help must tell at least one trustworthy person about what they have been feeling and what they have been doing now to make things better. The Blinks suggest this as it is essential that all children know that they have someone they can talk to and who they feel could be there for them in a time of need.

This rule also means that the Blinks feel happy that the child is no longer alone and so they can move on more readily to the next stage. As soon as each Blink feels confident that every child is supported by someone else, the circle of Blink magic is complete.

✓ This rule is probably the most important of the two. Children must never mention the Blinks' help. Children who have, cause the help to stop from that very moment when Blink magic was spoken about. If kept alive in the soul, Blinks' magic can glow deep within children providing gentle belief and positivity.

Stage 5... *Whey hey!* Once the Blinks have a sense of pleasure that their child has changed a difficult situation into a better one, a time of celebration begins. For seven whole days after the project has ended, starting at midnight the following day, much fun and reward begins.

At this stage, all the goodness that the Blinks have shared gets renewed through doing things that they enjoy. Some of the Blinks move across into other regions and holiday with other Blinks at this stage, some rest and some party in nearby meadows or parks, enjoying the natural nectar. Whatever they do, they do it to make them feel happy and rested, ready for their next exciting project.

Colin Confidence was happily waiting his turn to share his story. While he sat there he couldn't help but feel he should be with Nazim now so that his dreams weren't filled with the sadness of the day. He knew he couldn't start yet though, as him currently not talking was something Colin Confidence wasn't too confident with.

He started thinking about how working with children was hard enough without them not being able to tell you how they were feeling or evaluate how things are going. Suddenly a huge ripple of fear hit him and before he knew it he too couldn't speak, he had frozen and nothing was going to change this unless someone noticed and noticed quickly!

Chapter 7

The Thaw

Colin Confidence started swallowing hard. He began making light coughing noises to see if this was something to do with his vocal cords or his voice box. He could make some noises but when he tried to put his mouth into position to say something, he was unable to get the word out.

He nudged Flynn Fabulous who was sat by his side and pointed to his mouth.

Flynn Fabulous nodded and began looking in her leather bag that she wore across her chest. She pulled out a tiny pastille and handed it to Colin Confidence. You see, it is quite common for The Blinks to lose their voice due to all the talking they do and so restocking on throat medicine is quite normal.

Colin Confidence shook his head. His fear and frustration were obvious.

"What is it?" asked Flynn Fabulous. "Is your throat swollen?"

Colin Confidence shook his head ferociously.

"Here, write it down in my pad."

Colin Confidence took the pad and scribbled nervously, 'I can't speak'.

Flynn Fabulous stroked his arm, told

him to breathe calmly and told him she would interrupt the meeting so Colin Confidence could get the help and support he needed. She raised her arm but as she did, it was gently pushed downwards by someone standing behind her.

As she turned, she saw Blink 291216 Amber Awesome standing with Colin Confidence and beckoning her over too, out of the circle. "Oh thank goodness you noticed, Amber Awesome. Poor Colin Confidence has lost his ability to speak, please can you help him?"

Colin Confidence nodded with desperate eyes. He had never felt so scared, helpless, small or invisible.

"Indeed I can," replied Amber Awesome.

Colin Confidence's body dropped in a huge sigh of relief.

"First, I need you to hold on to how this feels, Colin Confidence. I need you to store the negative feelings inside you as they will be helpful to you later. So, shut your eyes and let the waves of fear and frustration wash around," said Amber Awesome.

Colin Confidence did as he was told and found himself change from a quivering Blink to a stronger self. He had ridden the emotional rollercoaster and survived.

Flynn Fabulous looked on fascinated by what she had just seen.

"Are you okay?" Amber Awesome asked.

Colin Confidence nodded. He knew he felt fine but he was nervous to see if he had recovered his voice.

"You will be able to speak now because it wasn't a fault in you that stopped you talking, it was something that I did to you," began Amber Awesome.

Flynn Fabulous gasped in shock.

Colin Confidence shook his head in disbelief and leaked out a "Why?" at the same time as feeling a huge relief when he realised he could talk again.

"I overheard you talking earlier about the young person that you want to work with but how you didn't feel like you knew enough about the situation. I took away your voice to give you the chance to truly feel how he is feeling, as that way we can help much more by understanding what each child is really going through," explained Amber Awesome.

Colin Confidence smiled. "Thank you so much. Although I didn't enjoy that, I have learnt more from that experience than I think anyone could have told me in words. Not being able to talk made me feel so weak, anxious and unimportant. That must be how Nazim has felt for a long time. He will have my greatest respect and focus because I only felt that for about 15 minutes and it was horrible. He has felt this for many years."

"Good. The exercise was a success. If I had told you I was going to do it, it would not have had the same impact. Some of the most difficult things in life teach us the most," smiled Amber Awesome. "Are you happy to share what has just happened with the rest of the Blinks at Stage 1?"

"Yes, of course," replied Colin Confidence.

"Come on then, let's do this," and all three Blinks had a group hug then headed back to the chocolate éclair tray.

As they arrived, Blink 1748 Ken Kindness was finishing pitching for the young person he had been observing and the Blinks were all cheering at the thought of another child being moved out of difficulty and into happier times. Amber Awesome moved to the front to take her spot as a Wise One while Colin Confidence and Flynn Fabulous went back to their positions in the circle.

"Wow, that was amazing," whispered Flynn Fabulous. "You were amazing!"

Colin Confidence gave a shy smile, as he was still partly recovering and hadn't got his true self back yet. However, for the first time in his life as a Blink, this feeling warmed him as it made him feel closer to Nazim. It had also activated a familiar feeling of when he was a much younger Blink and didn't feel like he deserved his Blink title. He was glad that he had tapped into some of the emotions that are deep within us all. This thought also gave him more confidence that he could help Nazim tap into his more positive emotions too.

Colin Confidence then got the chance to share his story of what he had noticed over the last few days with Nazim and what he had learned from Amber Awesome. The Blinks became speechless in wonder at what they were hearing and learning, and it was agreed that Nazim would get the support he so desperately needed.

Amber Awesome called the meeting to a close and thanked all the Blinks who had found young people to work with and wished them luck for their projects.

Remaining Blinks were hugged farewell from Stage 1 and sent off with oodles of excitement for their movement to Stage 2!

Now it was time for the sugar dough buffet to be created for all the Blinks to enjoy. Colin Confidence felt ready for action and was tempted to head over to Nazim's straight away. This would not have been wise though and deep down he knew it. Without refuelling, it could affect his skills and ability and this was not something he was going to risk.

Colin Confidence chatted away with the other Stage 1 Blinks whilst magically creating sweet delights out of what you and I wouldn't even be able to see. As they all celebrated together, Colin Confidence couldn't help but feel distracted and his heart was being pulled. He grabbed a couple of fancies and popped them into his rucksack.

"I need to go to Nazim's house," Colin Confidence told Flynn Fabulous. "Wish me luck because as we know, starting and finishing projects is always the hardest part."

"You don't need luck, Colin Confidence. You now have understanding and that is worth more than gold. Go and be brilliant because you are brilliant," beamed Flynn Fabulous.

Colin Confidence headed out of the bakery and into the night but how was he going to help Nazim if he didn't speak? That was the million pound question!

Chapter 8

Actions speak louder than words

Colin Confidence climbed through the letterbox of Nazim's house, being careful to not wake Wilf, the sleeping puppy. They had named their new dog Wilf as he was very wilful, which meant he liked doing what he liked doing and when he liked doing it!

Mr and Mrs Alam had bought him as a present for Nazim's birthday and hoped that by having someone special who he could love and play with and who would love him, this might move some of Nazim's difficulties on and allow him to develop more self-confidence.

It seemed to work at the beginning. Wilf

was good for Nazim. He made him laugh at some of the naughty things he did, like hide socks and jump into plant pots to eat the soil! The first walk with Wilf got all the family out together which was rare but very exciting.

Nazim was nervous about holding the lead at first and Wazidul and Rukkiah fed his insecurity because they wanted to hold Wilf's lead too. They told him he wouldn't be strong enough or that he might hurt Wilf by pulling his lead too tight.

Luckily, Mr and Mrs Alam noticed what they were doing and stopped them but the seed had been planted in Nazim's mind, and so the nervousness began. Sadly the whole dog walking experience became even more difficult due to the cuteness of Wilf and the many people who wanted to stop and fuss him. Nazim hated this. He couldn't answer when people asked his name and he froze when people asked how old he was. He even overheard one older lady walk away saying, "What a lovely friendly puppy, shame he belongs to such a rude child."

Nazim never wanted to walk Wilf after that. It was all too much attention and being shy made that very difficult. As Colin Confidence passed Wilf sleeping soundly in his comfy bed, he hoped that he could become part of nudging Nazim to a better place. In fact, he almost felt like he had gained Wilf's approval, as he was sure that the puppy had opened his eyes and winked at Colin Confidence as he was looking at him!

Dawn was just starting to break as Colin Confidence moved from the sleepy kitchen and up the stairs. Some gentle snoring could be heard from Mum and Dad's room and he was sure it was Mrs Alam. As he entered Nazim's room, light from the morning sun was just starting to break into the room from behind his blackout blind.

Nazim was sleeping but he suddenly began moving frantically in his dream and was thrashing around his bed, wrestling with his duvet like it was a wild animal and he was the hunter. The reality of his dream was less heroic.

Nazim was running away with all his might as he had just been asked a question by someone on his table in school and the whole class had suddenly developed huge heads with huge eyes and were looking at him, waiting for him to answer.

This was his worst fear. Not the big heads and eyes, they just seemed silly. No, it was the thought of saying something with everyone looking at him and saying the wrong thing, or worse, not being able to say anything at all. What Nazim hadn't yet learned, and this was part one of Colin Confidence's action plan, was that it wasn't what he did or didn't do that filled him with dread, it was more to do with what he thought other people thought of him at that time. It was his imagination that created a lot of his thoughts and these thoughts had created lots of negative feelings.

Colin Confidence sat waiting attentively, thinking how best to introduce himself. Should he go for the funny introduction as this might ease more fears? But then would Nazim take him seriously? This was certainly a serious issue! What about the hide and seek version to give Nazim the time he needed to get used to what was happening? Maybe being heard before being seen might be the best way, as that might make Nazim think that Colin Confidence was a bit shy too. Yes, that was what he would do.

As the clock moved through the dawn hours, Nazim also began to ease out of sleep and into wakefulness. Colin Confidence prepared himself for Stage one. He tiptoed over to Nazim's pillow and perched himself on the outer top edge.

"Morning Nazim, please don't be afraid. I am Colin Confidence. I am hoping that we can become very good friends and that

I can help you overcome some of your shyness so that you feel happier with your life."

Nazim hadn't moved, so Colin Confidence wasn't sure if he had heard what he had just said. He decided to move a little closer to his ear.

"Nazim, don't be alarmed. I am Colin Confidence and I would like you to know that I have been watching you closely lately and I want to help you with your shyness. If you will let me, that is?"

Still no movement from Nazim.

Colin Confidence decided to peep around Nazim's ear and see if he could see whether his eyes were open or closed. As he tilted his head, he could see that Nazim's eyes were as wide as could be and he was staring with an opened mouth up towards his ceiling.

Colin Confidence wasn't sure if Nazim had done the usual gulp, gulp, blink, which was how most children responded

to a first meeting. He tiptoed into the air
so that he was within Nazim's vision.

Nazim bolted out of bed and ended up in
a pile on the floor.

"Hey Nazim, it's okay. I am not someone
to fear, though I am sure that you feel
this is weird. I am Blink 24399 Colin
Confidence and it is my job to help
children who are having a difficult time
and you, Nazim, have won in the Blink
lottery because my help is available to you

and it's free!"

Nazim's eyes dipped slightly. He had never won anything before so it seemed like something special and good. Colin Confidence thought this was a good sign and so continued.

"I went to a special meeting last night and something strange happened to me so that I could help you more."

Nazim's expression changed to one of curiosity.

"I had my voice removed so that I could truly understand how things feel for you. It was so hard not feeling able to speak. I felt small, scared and helpless."

Nazim nodded. He felt those things every day.

"I wanted to help you but I was a little bit worried that I didn't know enough about your shyness and silence to help as best as I could. One of the older, wiser Blinks showed me by enabling me to experience it and that feeling is locked inside me now, so I can understand where you are coming from, Nazim."

Nazim's mouth moved slightly. What Colin Confidence had said just then made him feel a nice feeling in his tummy.

"Do you want us to do some work together, Nazim?" asked Colin Confidence.

Nazim's head moved slightly forward.

"Right, well the first thing I need you to understand is that your shyness isn't the dreadful thing that you think it is. It need not be your enemy anymore. Shyness is a very charming quality that makes the world a better place. If we were all overly confident in social situations, then nobody would get a word in! Shyness balances that out and is a strong wonderfulness that sometimes gets forgotten in our extrovert (outgoing) society but we, Nazim, are going to change that. Are you in?"

Nazim smiled and nodded definitely. No-one had ever made him feel that being shy could be a good thing. It had only ever been labelled as a bad thing and that made him feel bad.

"Can we shake on it then?" Colin Confidence held out his small hand towards Nazim.

This actually scared Nazim quite a lot. To shake on this meant he had made a promise, something he avoided at all costs as it could be another reason to feel like a failure if it didn't work.

"We won't change things overnight, Nazim, but we won't give up until we get you where you want to be. That's my promise to you," explained Colin Confidence, sensing Nazim's nervousness.

Nazim lifted his hand from his side and raised it in the direction of Colin Confidence. Millimetres became centimetres and slowly the distance was gone. As Nazim touched the tiny Blink's hand, he felt a ripple of magical excitement erupt in his tummy. What was it about this small fluffy creature that made him feel safe and not so alone?

Colin Confidence squealed in delight which made Nazim giggle and was the first sound that he had made in over 36 hours. This couldn't have been a better start, thought Colin Confidence and as we all know, now the real work could begin!.

Chapter 9

The power of mime!

Colin Confidence knew that the time was approaching when Mum would start getting Nazim up and ready for school.

"For the next week your target for overcoming your shyness is to change what you think about being shy. So, I'd like you to say to yourself, *'My shyness isn't a horrible thing, it means I am sensitive and caring'*, rather than, *'I hate being shy it makes me look weak and pathetic"*. Can you do that?"

Nazim looked at Colin Confidence. One half of him felt like he could and the other half thought that he couldn't. In one way, he was pleased that Colin Confidence hadn't asked him to start talking, as that already felt like it was going to be difficult given he hadn't been doing it for a while.

Could he really do this? It was *only* thinking. The problem was he really didn't believe he could. He really hated his shyness. He hated how it made him feel, what it made him do and what he thought it made other people think about him. He really wanted to ask Colin Confidence how it could work but then he remembered the handshake. He had said he would try things and sealed it with the shake so he had to try it and he really did want this to change.

Colin Confidence prompted Nazim again and just like a mind reader, he answered Nazim's questions.

"You are probably thinking that I am asking you to start saying something to yourself that doesn't feel like the truth and so how can that possibly work? Right?"

Nazim, who was still lying on the floor on top of his scrunched up yellow duvet, answered with a nod. He was unable to look at Colin Confidence as he felt like he had just been exposed and this made him feel very embarrassed.

"The brain is a funny thing, Nazim. It can get caught up in lots of thinking patterns. If we hold on to them and give them lots of attention, they can turn into feelings and then into beliefs."

Nazim scrunched his face as if to challenge that thought. He still didn't quite believe it. Colin Confidence knew he needed more information.

"A few years ago at one of our midnight meetings, Chief Blink did something to show us how important it is to help children change what they are thinking in order to change what they feel."

Nazim looked a bit surprised.

"Oh, the midnight meeting is where all the Blinks gather for guidance from each other and to refuel with the celebration banquet," explained Colin Confidence.

Nazim nodded, thankful that Colin Confidence was so good at reading his body language and facial expressions.

"So, Chief Blink got two Blinks (who were known for being good throwers and catchers) and asked them to stand on the counter ready to throw a piece of squidged up doughnut to each other as fast as they could. She then asked the rest of us to count how many times the ball was passed from one side to the other, whilst Blink 30321 Terry Try-Your-Best filmed the whole thing."

Nazim's eyes widened. This sounded interesting.

"We all focussed on the ball and everyone was counting our heads moving with the ball. After about 10 minutes, when Chief Blink noticed all our heads moving together, she stood directly in the middle of where the ball was being thrown and started dancing in a silly way. She danced like a funky chicken, like a disco goddess and strutted like an Ancient Egyptian!"

Nazim put his hands to his mouth to try and stop himself from laughing.

"It's okay to laugh, Nazim. We all did! Anyway, after two minutes, Chief Blink stopped and went back to the side of the counter. We all continued to count the ball. After a further eight minutes, Chief Blink told the Blinks to stop throwing and catching."

Nazim was really engrossed in the story now and even flickered his eyes several times towards Colin Confidence and was met with kind, gentle and honest eyes.

"Chief Blink then asked us, the counting Blinks, how many times the ball of doughnut had been passed."

Nazim raised his eyes in curiosity.

"7543 was shouted. 7498 said another. 7552 exclaimed someone else. The number was irrelevant in this experiment.

Nazim lifted his arms and lowered his brow as if to say, *'How can the number be irrelevant?'*

"You too are probably thinking, how can the number not matter? That was the whole point of the exercise, right? Well, let me explain further."

Nazim had his head tilted downwards but was looking directly towards Colin Confidence, while hiding as much of his eye under the canopy of his eyelid and lashes.

"Chief Blink asked how many Blinks had noticed something different in the middle of the throwing and catching. There were probably 100 Blinks counting, Nazim, how many do you think noticed Chief Blink dancing?"

Nazim raised his shoulders as if to say, '*I don't know.*'

"Go on have a guess. More than half?"

Nazim shrugged and nodded a half smile as if to say, '*more than likely*'. He really didn't like being putting on the spot as that meant he could be wrong.

"Less than half?"

Nazim raised his shoulders again in a quick jerk but most definitely shook his head too.

"The answer, Nazim, is one! One Blink noticed Chief Blink dancing."

Nazim opened his mouth in amazement and widened his eyes in disbelief.

"Yes, it's amazing isn't it. It was only Blink 24317 Alice Aim-High who had noticed Chief Blink and it was because she had lost count so at that time, wasn't giving all of her attention to the doughnut ball being passed."

Nazim was most definitely surprised by this. His eyebrows looked like they were about to leave his face!

"I know. I couldn't believe I hadn't noticed it either. It was only when Chief Blink hung a white paper bag from the bread shelf and projected the film onto it, that we all saw what we had missed!"

Nazim was shaking his head in disbelief. He was sure he would have seen it.

"Everyone thinks they will see it, Nazim, until you do it. I am sure there are experiments on the internet if you want to give it a try. It is called *perceptual blindness* and it shows how we can all miss what is right in front of us if we are concentrating on something else."

Nazim quickly ran to his desk and scribbled the words *'perceptual blindness'* down on his pad. He would most definitely have a look at that later.

"I once worked with a girl called Jenny, who was convinced she had a horrible nose. She began thinking this a couple of times a week, then every day and before she knew it, that was all she thought about. All her attention had gone on how dreadfully big and ugly her nose was. Her *perception* (opinion or thought) of her nose had become so strong that she was blinded to anything else."

Nazim nodded in a way that showed he got the idea. In fact, he was starting to see where Colin Confidence was going with the whole idea of changing what he thought about his shyness. He spent too many hours a day hating being shy and frustrated at the way his shyness made him feel.

"Jenny didn't see how amazing her eyes were or how pretty her whole face was when these features were put together, or how lovely her nose actually was."

Nazim's shoulders dropped. He did this a lot and recognising this made him feel sad.

"Hey, don't be too hard on yourself, Nazim. You haven't done anything wrong here. This is something every brain does. It is not a sign of failure."

Nazim was too down-hearted to feel that this could be true. In his head, he had done this for years and felt he was stupid because of it.

"Anyway, once Jenny realised what she was doing, she was able to change it and pay less attention to her nose. It was difficult at first. The thoughts just kept flooding in. However, with practice she changed the time she allowed herself to think these negative thoughts about her nose and eventually she felt her nose was okay. So, if Jenny can do it, Nazim, so can you."

Nazim was starting to feel that Colin Confidence was wrong here. He knew he was different. Yet for the first time in his whole life, a new dialogue kept popping into his head which made him feel it was worth giving it a try. He remembered the handshake. He had to try at least. Nothing would change if he didn't allow himself to try something different.

Nazim smiled up at Colin Confidence. Although he felt scared and worried about getting this wrong, he stayed focussed on what was being asked of him. Today he was going to see if he could weaken his negative thoughts about his shyness. As he thought this, Colin Confidence noticed his shoulders lift and his chest inflate. He already looked more positive.

"Well done, Nazim. You have made a great start. Now remember, think differently to feel differently and reduce the time you think negative thoughts about your shyness. You are an ace kid who is sensitive, kind and thoughtful and that is the beauty of shyness."

Colin Confidence heard Mum and Wilf

coming up the stairs to wake Nazim for the day. "I will check in with you later. You can do this. I know you can."

Nazim watched Colin Confidence tiptoe out through the window and then was engulfed with puppy licks of adoration from Wilf.

"What are you doing on the floor?" asked Mum.

Even if he was talking, how on earth would Nazim explain that!

Chapter 10

Shoo shyness shoo

As Nazim ate his breakfast that morning, he wondered how the weeks ahead might unfold. Several times he found himself wondering whether Colin Confidence had actually been there or if it was a very realistic dream.

Mum sidled up beside him and pulled in a chair. "I am worried about you Nazim, do I need to be?"

Nazim looked downwards from the corner of his eyes just as he usually did whenever anyone asked him a question.

"You have always been quiet, but this is taking it to a whole new level. You have hardly said a word for days."

It wasn't that he had *hardly* said a word, he **hadn't** said a word. Nazim felt sad that Mum didn't know that.

"Answer your mum when she is talking to you, Nazim. Stop being so rude when your mum is talking to you. This shyness is getting ridiculous it makes you seem ignorant, disrespectful and as if you can't be bothered with people."

Mum shot Dad one of her usual stares.

"Ignore your dad, Nazim. He is being very insensitive and unkind. For goodness sake Mo, you said you were shy when you were younger. Give him a break!"

"Yes, I was and I hated it. I was scared of doing anything new, worried about being easily embarrassed, fearful of being rejected by people and, worst of all, dreaded saying something out loud and it be wrong or I started mumbling. It affected me every day of my life as a child. I locked myself into my shyness too long. I do not want that for my son."

Nazim thought about what Colin Confidence had said that morning. 'Maybe Dad used to do the same thing as me,' he wondered, thinking his dad might have spent a lot of time focussing on negative thoughts about his own shyness. 'Maybe Dad is doing it again right now because I am, maybe it's on his mind again.'

Nazim looked at his dad and felt sorry for him a little bit. His journey sounded hard. Hopefully though, Colin Confidence was going to ease it for him. What worried him most was that Mum had just told Dad he was all the things that Colin Confidence had told Nazim he wasn't.

Dad was insensitive, Nazim was sensitive. Dad was unkind, Nazim was kind and thoughtful. Dad was forceful whilst Nazim was gentle. Suddenly and for the first time in his life, Nazim saw his shyness as being better than the alternative. Was this the start of him accepting who he was rather than rejecting it?

Nazim remembered his target, to challenge his negative thinking about his shyness. Yes, he had just done just that. He could proudly tell Colin Confidence this when he saw him later. With this new found feeling of pride, he put on his shoes and got ready for school.

On the way, he was thinking how easy today's target had been. He was also amazed how good he felt from succeeding. As he approached the crossing, he felt the presence of some people behind him.

"Hey, have you brought Nazim's remote control again today?" asked one of the voices.

"Yes, I have it here. It was so funny pressing mute yesterday and keeping him quiet. Wonder if we can change his channel too?" queried the other child. Then they both started laughing and shoulder-barged past him, turning around to point and sneer even more.

Nazim felt sick. Like two thieves, the

boys had robbed him in broad daylight of the positive feeling he had just felt. Before he knew it, his mind was bombarding him with all the things he hated about being shy.

Colin Confidence appeared from nowhere. "Are you doing it?"

Nazim looked totally fed up. He could hardly walk, never mind challenge some of his deepest thoughts.

"Come on, you shook on it! You promised you would try. I know this morning you felt like you had reached your target. But the targets I set, Nazim, don't end when you have done them just once. They are not like goals that you can tick off and say job done! They are skills that become values about who you are as a person. The more you do them the more natural they will become."

Nazim thought that sounded reasonable even though he was a bit gutted that this needed a lot more effort than he first realised.

"Also, those children were in the wrong, not you. They were being mean and wanted to affect how you felt. You let them win. That feeling you had this morning is not for them to take away, or for you to give away. Not if you don't want to anyway! Can you remember the good feeling you had this morning?"

Nazim put on a serious thinking face. If he thought hard, he could just about feel the remaining drops that had not yet faded. He gave a weak nod.

"Right. It takes 11 seconds to lock in a positive feeling so that we make it last longer. So, focus on that feeling and whilst you are giving it all your thinking and attention, remind yourself what it is and why it is there."

Nazim looked confused.

"Say to yourself by repeating each sentence after me:

✓ *I have started changing how I think today and that makes me feel good.*

✓ *I know that I am in charge of how much attention I give to my thoughts.*

✓ *I will not see my shyness as an enemy anymore.*

✓ *I am a good person and being shy makes me a better person, not a failure."*

Nazim did as he was told. Each sentence he repeated brought the good feeling back and made it feel stronger.

"It is really important to remember, Nazim, that your personal targets actually have the biggest impact when things seem difficult. When somethings feels hard to do that is when we need to try the hardest. That is when we start making the bigger changes."

Nazim could see that and so nodded to show his understanding.

"So, today will be tough. You are

changing how your brain thinks. You are creating new happier brain pathways and beginning to destroy older, negative ones. It's a big job, but you can do it. Think of them as mini experiments. Just remember it isn't a one time target, these are forever focuses.

Nazim nodded enthusiastically. This was day one and he had a lot to do, but it would all be worth it in the end when he diluted his shyness, and became happier too.

He watched the two boys scampering off into the school gates and his heart sank again. So did his shoulders.

"Don't let them have it, Nazim. It is your special feeling. Laugh it off. Think of what they said as funny. Imagine if we had remote controls, we could use them on each other and change what people do. What mischief we could all get into with that! Well, I certainly wouldn't have a job for a start as I could just change your thought channel, Nazim, and that would be everything sorted."

Nazim smiled and imagined what he could get Wilf to do if he had such power. He also wished it could be that easy but somehow, he knew that nothing could be learned if that was the case. He knew he had a lot to learn and although that made him feel scared, it also made him feel excited. His shoulders stood proud again.

"Good work, Nazim! You look strong again. Even if we don't feel it, sometimes we must act it to become it. This changes the messages we send to the brain. When our shoulders are down, it pulls on our neck muscles which then makes our face muscles drop. That adds stress to the side of the head, which makes us feel stressed and anxious. When we straighten our shoulders, we loosen the muscles in our neck and face and then we feel more confident and relaxed. We might not feel it, but we can fake it until we feel it. It sounds like magic, but it isn't!"

Nazim pushed his shoulders back further and touched the muscles in his lower jaw. Colin Confidence was right, they felt so much less tight and tense.

"Are you ready? I will never be too far away, not for a while anyway. Look at everything you have already done in this short space of time since we have known each other. You are amazing! I knew you were ripe and ready for this," said Colin

Confidence with a genuine smile of pride.

As nervous as Nazim felt, those shoulders were going to stay back and his mind was going to stay focussed on the positive things about who he was.

Without saying a word, he put his thumb up in the air with a determination that spoke volumes. But could a thumbs up see him through the challenges of what lay ahead?

Chapter 11

Fight!

The first half of the week went well for Nazim. Breakfast time had not been too problematic, well no more than normal. Wazidul and Rukkiah found just as many reasons to point fun at him and so Mum found more reasons to stop them. Dad seemed to have eased off the pressure that Nazim always felt was directed at him and which led him to feeling even more of a failure as a son.

Getting to school had been a bonus too, as Mum was going into work slightly later and as it was on the way, she could drop him off. Nazim liked having some time with just him and Mum, as he felt she understood him more than anyone else.

"You look brighter today, Nazim. Have you slept well?" asked Mum.

Nazim shook his head in a *not really* sort of way.

"I have had a word with your dad about the frustration he feels with your shyness. You know, Nazim, he spent many years being shy and so it pains him to see you suffering like he used to."

Nazim knew about his dad's shyness only too well. He was reminded of it every day when his shyness stopped him doing something that Dad felt he should do.

"He loves you so much. It is hard for both of us to watch you fade away at times and not seem to want the friends or the party invitations that other children seem to share. I just wish you could tell us how you feel about things sometimes, so that we're not always guessing."

Nazim looked into his mum's sad eyes and smiled a downward sad smile.

"Will you think about talking to me, Nazim? Just me and you? I'd like to hear your thoughts and feelings, so I can understand how to support you better."

Nazim nodded. He felt that if he chose not to talk for much longer, he may well lose the confidence and ability in this area that most of us take for granted. He also had a flash back of Colin Confidence earlier that morning and couldn't help but think how valuable talking with him would be!

"Oh thank you, Nazim. How about I pick you up from after school club tonight and we go and have a hot chocolate with whipped cream and marshmallows at the café? We can talk about it all. Just me and you without any interruptions. Deal?" asked Mum hopefully.

In Nazim's head two things were going on. One side of his brain was suggesting he never speak again, refuse every offer of help and support and stay hidden from the scary, busy world for as long

as possible. However, since meeting
Colin Confidence, new thoughts were
bombarding his brain.

Nazim was reminded that he didn't like
feeling like this. He felt that change was
now a possibility, especially with the help
of Colin Confidence. For the first time
ever, this wasn't about him hating his
shyness, it was about him accepting it and
learning how to use it to his advantage.
His shyness was not going to be his enemy
anymore, but a friend who he was going to
get to know better.

"D..," said Nazim automatically but was
quickly silenced by his protective brain.
"De..," he continued but that was as far as
he could go that time.

"Oh Nazim, thank you so much. Is that
a deal then?"

Further conflict occurred in his head.
Yes. No. Yes. No. Yes. No. He began to
wonder which would win. Yes.

Nazim nodded. He knew yes had to win

out. It was the only way change was going to happen. Mum grabbed his hand and squeezed it with love, pride and relief.

"I will be there about 5.15pm. I am so excited, my beautiful boy. I have missed you so much."

Nazim felt nervous. It would have been much easier to say nothing or no but Colin Confidence had activated a new thought system in his head, which he felt was more important and useful and needed to be listened to.

As Nazim unclicked his seatbelt to exit the car, Mum reached over and cupped his face. "You are so wonderful Nazim. You are kind, gentle and sensitive, qualities that make you very special, never forget that."

Nazim looked shocked. He had heard similar words already that morning from Colin Confidence. Had Mum said them before and he had not registered them? Was this a bit like hearing a new word for the first time and then suddenly people are saying it around you all the time?!

Nazim walked into school. His thoughts at that time felt positive. Maybe he wasn't the stupid, weak, pathetic, dull, boring person that he thought he was. Maybe he could be seen as quiet, gentle and thoughtful.

Suddenly, another brain battle began. It felt like the two sides of his brain were squaring up to fight. A mental argument began:

Negative shy brain, 'Are you having a laugh? You will never be anything other than *Nothing to say Nazim.* You will always be shy so get used to it.'

Positive shy brain, 'Whoa, that's a bit harsh. So, does that mean only confident popular kids are important? Who made up that rule?'

Negative shy brain, 'Yes it does and they made it up! Unless you are funny, popular, exciting and noticed, the world will pass you by. Life is a ticket only ride so if you don't get one, you miss the excitement. Nazim will never get a ticket so get used to it.'

Positive shy brain, 'That is total rubbish. Can you imagine how hard it would be being the friend of someone who was always wanting attention and excitement? It would be awful. We need our friends to listen when we need them, care about us and stop sometimes to see what is going on around us. A shyer friend notices everything that is going on. They will always be there for you.'

Negative shy brain, 'No, no, that's rubbish. You must be like them to fit in, you must be better. Nazim will never be.'"

Positive shy brain, 'Why? Who said it is us that should change? Maybe the loud, attention grabbing people need to step back a bit and become more like us? Maybe we would all be better being somewhere in the middle?'

Negative shy brain, 'Wrong, wrong, wrong. Nazim is who he is. Don't try to fight it. Stay quiet, stay hidden, stay safe.'

Positive shy brain, 'You will not win with me, negative shy brain. We will not be a slave to such thinking any more. Nazim has a choice now, just wait and see.'

Nazim trudged into school already exhausted at the mental conversation which had just hijacked his brain. It really did feel like two parts of his brain were at loggerheads with each other and he was in the middle.

He remembered Colin Confidence

saying that at first it would be difficult to challenge some of your normal thoughts, but he never expected it to be as difficult as this. He suddenly remembered the dancing Chief Blink story. This was what he needed to do. Not give as much attention to his negative thinking brain and instead give more attention to his positive thinking brain! That was already proving easier said than done!

The mental fights went on all day. This is the scoreboard of results for situations that day:

Situation	Negative-Brain	Positive brain
Answering the register	1	0
Getting into assembly	0	1
Changing what he thought people thought about him	1	0
Being kind to himself	0	1

Situation	Negative-Brain	Positive brain
Having eye contact with people on his table	1	0
Reducing the negative thinking about his shyness	0	1
Talking to people	1	0
Aggregate score	*4*	*3*

By the end of the day, Nazim was shattered. As he walked to after school club with his hands in his pockets and his shoulders leading the way, he felt a softness tickling the palm of his hand.

He jolted his arm in distress. There on the end of his thumb, hanging on with all his might, was Colin Confidence.

"Hi, Nazim. Sorry, I didn't mean to shock you. I have been trying to get your attention with a few *'psssts'*, but you were so focussed on your thoughts that you didn't hear me. Can you sit out here for a while before you go into after school club?"

Nazim nodded. This was no problem at all. He usually sat under the covered area once the adults knew he was there, as it was quiet and he felt quite safe and unnoticed.

"Busy day, Nazim? How has it gone?"

Nazim slumped.

"Hey, it is only day one. I told you this morning that it would be tough at the beginning, but it does get easier. Are you ready to talk yet?"

Nazim really didn't have much energy left to hold his head up, never mind to talk. He shook his head.

"Okay. No problem. Could you tap once for yes and two for no instead?"

That seemed a better option and so Nazim agreed. It was also a step closer to communicating with Mum later too.

"Have you worked on your targets

today?"

Nazim tapped once.

"Has it been difficult?"

Nazim tapped one very loud tap.

"You have worked really hard today. You will be very tired."

Another very loud tap.

"Well done, Nazim. You have started changing how your brain works. Today you have started new brainwaves which will eventually become brain pathways. It all starts with thinking differently. Have you challenged some negative thoughts today?"

Nazim tapped another single tap.

"Did that feel good?"

Nazim tapped a single tap once more.

"Did your normal brain shut up when it was challenged?"

Nazim thumped down twice on the

wooden bench.

"It won't give up on the first day, Nazim. That part of your brain has been in charge for many months, maybe years, it will take time to weaken but it sounds like you have made a great start. So, do you feel proud of yourself?"

Nazim tapped two taps.

"Does it feel like your negative brain has still won today, even after all the hard work?"

Nazim tapped a weak, sad tap.

"Did that part of your brain score more wins today?"

Tap.

"Is it saying lots of negative things to you now, such as, *'you can't change, you won't change?'*"

Tap.

"Okay, so what can you do now?"

Nazim didn't know a number for *don't know* so lifted his shoulders.

"You can either roll over, agree and give up. Or you can remind yourself of all you have done today and even up the scores. You might not feel the effects today but if you stick at it, by the end of the week you could start feeling much happier. Are you going to keep at it? Do we have a deal?"

Nazim forgot where he was and the familiarity of the conversation from that morning led him to reply, "Deal."

Colin Confidence yelped in happiness.

Nazim looked shocked and very scared. He was working towards doing this with Mum, but not now. He was worried that he had now broken his pact with himself and terrified he may have made the worst choice ever. He tightened his lips.

"Hey, speaking is a sign of success not failure. You are two points up in your positive brain by pushing yourself and challenging those negative thoughts. If you can find the strength to do that now, I am sure the score for today will be a win to you."

Nazim knew Colin Confidence was right. No way was he going to give up now. That would lead nowhere fast. He also knew that releasing the grip of silence could only speed up the journey and direction. Inside his head Nazim felt a ripple of relief. He had tipped the aggregate score from 4:3 to 4:5 and it produced a feeling he had never felt before, one which released a beaming smile.

"Yes. Day one a Nazim success," beamed Colin Confidence. "Are you ready for day two?"

"Y...eee...sss!" replied Nazim and they high fived!

"Right, if you can do it now, you can do it anytime. The values you have - determination, courage and motivation - are what have led to today being a positive day. Yet these values have always been and will always be inside you. I can only make suggestions, Nazim. You have done all the hard work. Hurray! It is 5pm and I am going to leave you for now, as your mum will be here soon. Keep up the good work and I will check-in again soon. Remember, I am never too far away but you are doing the work Nazim, not me."

Nazim leaned back on the bench. He had so much to think about and so much to do. His next challenge was talking to Mum about all this without mentioning Colin Confidence. However, after the amount of fight rounds he had done in his brain already today, this challenge seemed the easiest of them all!

Chapter 12

The power of marshmallows

On the way to the café, Nazim leaned his head on the window of the car, milling over all the things that had happened over the last few days. It would have been very easy for someone to have convinced him that it had all been a weird but wonderful dream. It was only the gentle upturn of his mouth that made him realise that although things were difficult, his feelings were ever so slightly shifting in a better direction.

"How has your day been today Naz?" asked Mum as they sat looking at the crimson traffic light.

A gentle but positive squeak of, "Mmm" left Nazim's mouth.

"Oh brilliant, son. That is brilliant. What are you going to have at the café? Your usual?"

A longer slower, "Mmmmm" escaped from Nazim.

"You have loved a whipped cream hot chocolate with lots of marshmallows since you were a little boy. I remember the first time you tried the cream off the top of mine, you must have only been 15 months old. Do you remember it?"

"Nergh," replied Nazim. This was his simple verbal grunt which just meant no, as saying words out loud clearly still felt a huge jump for him. He was also still scared that it might bring him too much unwanted attention.

"We were in the park café with all the mums I had met at the new baby sessions. Do you remember Sarah, Vicky, Stacey, and Jayne?"

Nazim nodded with a single, "Mm".

"We had been for a walk around the park. Well, I say a walk, you were still tottering, as were most of the other children. It was quite a challenge to walk crouched over, holding your beautiful little hand whilst pushing the pushchair, and keeping watch on our older toddlers, who were confidently running off in any direction they could!"

Nazim laughed at the image of his smaller, younger self. Was the challenge of walking as hard as the challenges he was facing today?

"You would fall over all the time but it never stopped you trying. A gentle arm pull would steady you on your feet again. Oh, I miss those days."

Nazim laughed again with a warm, contented sound. Maybe Colin Confidence was right after all. The strength and determination was there inside him. He just needed to find it again and use it.

"So, after the walk we were all shattered.

We popped in the café for a drink, a well-deserved rest and a natter. I was at the front of the queue and ordered my hot chocolate with you squirming in my arms, yearning to be put down. I carried my drink over gently, tempting Rukkiah towards the table with a milk lolly. We perched on a wooden bench and the three of us were reading a book together.

Then Vicky shouted over to say she had forgotten her purse and asked if could I lend her five pounds. As I turned to get the purse out of my bag, you moved closer to the cream mountain. Without me realising, you began swiping cream and marshmallows off the top and into your mouth as quickly as possible. As I passed my purse to Vicky, the whole café was looking over and giggling. You had cream and marshmallows all over your face, hands and t-shirt! I have the photo at home somewhere. Ahh, those were the days."

Nazim felt warm and fluffy inside. He loved hearing stories of when he was a baby. Today was the first time he found himself looking at himself. He was quite envious of all the care his younger self had, everything just seemed easier then. Then he had another thought. Why had he just thought *had*? That made it seem like the care wasn't there now. He knew that it was, and today what he and Mum were doing together was a reminder of that. It wasn't that he had forgotten, it was just that he hadn't thought about it for a while. This thought was a good thought and it made him feel good.

They approached the car park and Mum turned off the engine. "Before we go inside Nazim, please can I ask a favour while we are sitting here on our own?"

Nazim looked at Mum and thought how pink-cheeked and lovely she looked. He nodded with another, "Mmm."

"Please will you just say Mum?"

Nazim was shocked to hear that this was the favour. His brain had imagined all kinds of possibilities.

"I haven't heard you say that word for a long time and I miss hearing it more than you realise. You are my baby boy, my precious baby boy and I am always here for you." She wiped a tear from the corner of her eye.

Nazim breathed in deeply. If she had asked him to say this at the start of the journey, he wasn't sure he could do it. It felt too big a step. However, the loveliness of the journey, the stories, warmth and love added the icing to a successful day. Could saying this one word be the cherry on the cake for both their days?

He breathed in deeply and shut his eyes. He rolled his tongue around his mouth. He stretched his lips wide and exposed his teeth. He realised he was doing verbal warm-ups.

Nazim took off his seatbelt and turned his body to look at Mum. His heart was racing and his mouth was dry. His hands started getting quite clammy. Do it! Do it! Do it! He kept repeating these words to himself.

He was surprised, because in the distance a much weaker thought was saying, "don't do it". This battle, though, had one outright winner. He breathed in one more deep breath.

"Mum. Thanks. You're the best."

Mrs Alam burst into tears and grabbed Nazim into her so tightly that he thought he might stop breathing. Hot, wet tears dripped onto him from above and onto Mum from him. It was a very soggy five minutes.

"Thank you, Nazim. Thank you so much. Whatever it is you are going through, I will always be here for you. No problem is too big for team Alam. Do you understand?"

Nazim nodded and they both wiped away tears from their eyes.

"Come on then, let's go and celebrate a good day with some serious hot chocolates."

Colin Confidence puffed up his dampened fluff. Mum was doing okay with Nazim and in fact, better than he had hoped but there were still a few things he needed to help her with.

Dad was where Colin Confidence now needed to focus his attention. There was a lot of work to do there. Tonight was going to be busy and he was going to need his brain spanner!

Chapter 13

Knowing me, knowing you

Nazim and Mum had a lovely time at the park café. The hot chocolates tasted chocolatier, creamier and marshmallowier than he had ever tasted. It all felt so warm and familiar; they had spent many a lunchtime there when he was little and the story in the car brought all those lovely feelings back. The conversation between them was simple but alive, well just about.

Mum kept asking questions. This prompted Nazim to answer with one word answers and simple sounds whenever he could get away with it. He thought about starting a conversation a few times, but he was so out of practice, it felt like a huge step. So, he tucked into his drink instead.

Just as they were about to leave, one of the mum friends arrived. They embraced each other with a hug and a kiss, as it had been a while since they met up. Sarah looked down at Nazim.

"Wow, look at you. Aren't you a handsome boy?"

Mrs Alam smiled and remarked how gorgeous he was, inside and out.

Nazim felt overwhelmed with the comment but lifted his head and smiled in the direction of the lovely, enthusiastic lady.

Mum beamed too. Normally, she felt a need to go into overdrive at times like this to distract the attention from Nazim as much as possible so her son didn't appear rude.

"What a smile too!" Sarah turned her head over her shoulder towards her own son. "This is Nazim. Do you remember him, Ellis? You two have known each other since you were months old and used to be really good buddies when you were little."

Nazim couldn't remember him, although he had a faint image of a dark-haired boy who never said very much. Regardless, they used to run around together sometimes.

"Come out Ellis, stop being so silly. I am so sorry. He is so shy that he really struggles in situations like this. It's a nightmare, to be honest. Ellis, come around please!"

Nazim knew how Ellis was feeling only too well. He had a similar jolt in his tummy in these situations too. He felt like he was watching himself. He wasn't sure what to do in this situation. Although he felt that Ellis probably wanted to be left alone, Nazim wondered if he craved someone to break through the shy world and smile at him anyway, rather than the negative-sounding, 'oh' which most people usually said.

Nazim peeped around Sarah's side and gave Ellis a smile. He wasn't confident enough to look him in the eye so wasn't sure if he had seen or smiled back. He then felt a huge surge of courage and whispered, "why does shy always sound so bad? Why can't we just be quiet? Everyone is quiet sometimes! Well, apart from our mums!"

Ellis laughed and looked in the direction of Nazim. For a millisecond, their eyes shared the same space. This was a connection of likeness that he had never experienced before.

"I know. I hate it. I always feel so rubbish as I can't do what everyone else seems to do so easily."

"Me neither. Trying to be normal seems like such hard work," said Nazim.

The mums were still chatting from above and so hadn't noticed the boys interacting, as that was the last thing either of them expected to happen.

"Why don't you two walk down to the playground, and we will follow in a minute?" suggested Sarah. "I am just getting a couple of pieces of apple cake for Grandma."

You can imagine that this was a big thing for both boys. Together, without anywhere to hide or anyone to save them from social awkwardness, could be horrific. Yet the boys knew these feelings only too well and both would apply no pressure so maybe it was worth a try.

"I will," said Nazim nervously.

Ellis smiled, "Okay".

So, they left the café with their hands in their pockets and their heads facing forwards, quite unsure of what to do next. Nazim looked back at his mum, worried he had made the wrong choice. He noticed her looking at him and nodding her head enthusiastically with her thumbs up, showing him he could do it.

"Have you always been shy?" asked

Ellis.

"Yes, much to the disappointment of my dad," replied Nazim. "He reminds me every day that I am missing out and come across as rude."

"My mum and dad both do that. My dad is still shy and it drives my mum mad.

She just doesn't get it. That is why she is always talking to other people. Me and my dad are more than happy to just sit quietly watching everything going on."

"Me too," shouted Nazim excitedly. Ellis got it, he really got it. This felt great.

The boys got to the playground and happily meandered from one piece of equipment to the other. Talking wasn't the expectation though, as much was communicated through silent competitiveness and laughs when one beat the other, especially on swinging as high as they could.

"Do you remember that time when we were little and we hid for ages in the bottom of the climbing frame? You had collected loads of pine cones and laid them all out like a prized collection. I had to keep guard, so no-one came and spoiled the display. Our mums were so cross when we turned up unaware of all the fuss," explained Ellis.

"Oh, yes I'd forgotten about that. Being told off in front of everyone was awful. I certainly don't think that helped our shyness," replied Nazim.

The boys both laughed.

"I wish having fun with people was as easy as that now," said Ellis. "Most of the boys in my class are so confident and popular that I feel pathetic next to them. They're not mean or anything, but I just don't feel like I fit in sometimes. Do you ever feel like that?"

"All the time. The boys in my year are the same, some of them are mean though. There are a few girls who are kind when I feel a bit left out, but I am just not like them. Sometimes I pretend to be the same but I am so rubbish at it, it makes things worse," responded Nazim.

"Yes, me too. I wish we were in the same school," said Ellis.

Nazim spent a few moments wondering what that would be like, to have someone who understood your shyness and didn't put pressure on you to be any different. Someone who took the sting out of being on your own in the playground. Another person to ease the awkwardness of always being alone.

"Yes, me too. Maybe we could meet up sometimes though. I'm sure our mums would be happy to see each other a bit more," said Nazim.

"That would be good, really good. Here they are now, let's ask them?" shouted Ellis running off in their direction.

As the boys started to become new old friends again, the mums were sharing stories of worry about their two beautiful but troubled boys. Both shed a tear of sadness as they sidled towards the park, linking arms in recognition of each other's concerns.

"Can Nazim come and play at ours sometime soon, Mum? Please? Please?"

Both mums looked at Nazim to check

it was something he really wanted to do. Nazim looked back with an excited nod.

"Yes, of course you can. That would be wonderful! We were hoping you two would hit it off and guess what? We have just found out you are both going to the same secondary school in September," exclaimed Mrs Alam.

The boys, just as shy boys do, nodded reservedly but inside, they were fist-punching the air.

The mums hugged and kissed goodbye and a plan was arranged for the following Saturday, when Nazim was to go to Ellis's for tea. The boys nodded in each other's direction with a new feeling of belonging. They had each met another member of the shy club and it felt like it could be the start of a good friendship.

On the way home, Mum told Nazim how proud she was of him. With Mum, he still felt that moving back into talking was unnatural and he wondered why it had been so much easier with Ellis. Maybe it was because he could be the newer Nazim with his friend, whereas Mum knew what had been going on for so long and that trapped him.

Either way, to move forward, this was something Nazim was going learn to accept.. He also felt that Ellis could not only be a huge help to him, but hopefully Colin Confidence's tips could be shared with Ellis too, almost like a buy one, get one free! As he watched the world pass by through the car window, he tried to put a name to what he was feeling. It wasn't happiness, or pride, although he knew they were tangled within it somewhere. It wasn't excitement either.

He wasn't even sure if he knew what it was called, so he asked. "Mum, what is the feeling when things about the future start to feel better and the fear is starting to fade?"

"Hope, my darling, that feeling is hope. It is one of the most wonderful and important feelings in the world and is essential for other positive feelings like happiness. I am feeling it too, Nazim. Whatever happened today to bring on this shift is like magic and we must appreciate it every second that we feel it. That way, it doesn't go away."

Hope. This was a new feeling and he liked it a lot. Was this anything to do with Colin Confidence? Could he be part of the magic? If so, what else might happen? Little did Nazim know, but the effects of the magic would make themselves clear over the next few days.

Chapter 14

Brain okey cokey!

While Nazim and the rest of his family slept in the deep of the night, the next stage of Colin Confidence's plan began. The helpful Blink made sure to exit tonight's midnight meeting promptly as there was so much to do.

He couldn't fault Nazim. He had made great progress in the short space of time they had known each other. This was usually the case for the Blinks. Children and young people's brains are so flexible that they can take in new information and develop so quickly. That's what always makes them a pleasure to work with.

Adults can sometimes be more difficult. Have you heard the saying, *'You can't teach an old dog new tricks*? Colin Confidence thought for a minute about Wilf. In the eight weeks the puppy had been a part of the family, the tricks they had taught him were:

- ✓ sit
- ✓ give paw
- ✓ lie down
- ✓ answer to his name
- ✓ stop eating the soil out of the plant pots
- ✓ tell them when he wanted to go to the toilet
- ✓ walk on a lead
- ✓ fetch
- ✓ go into his bed

This was all very important as after 20 weeks of age, puppies' brains become slightly less trainable and so all the hard work needs to be done while they are young. It is similar with children, though we do have lots more years!

So tonight, he was going to work on the older brains and his brain spanner was going to come in handy. He decided to work in order from the least needed tweaks to the most. Rukkiah would be first.

Colin Confidence perched on her pillow as she slept soundly. From out of his rucksack he pulled an extendable plastic, telescope-like device. This was made of the softest, thinnest plastic and was gentle enough to sit in her ear so that positive messages about Nazim could be planted. He then removed a tiny thought machine which he had spent the day loading with things Rukkiah needed to hear about Nazim. He pressed play and let the messages do the work in Rukkiah's deep-sleeping mind.

Next was Wazidul. He needed slightly

more than Rukkiah. He needed a thought filter adding and this was a trickier operation. The hardest part about this manoeuvre for a Blink was getting the person in the right sleeping position, on their back. Luckily, as Colin Confidence entered the room, Wazidul had just flopped into that position. His mouth was slightly open which also made it easier.

This needed to happen quickly. Colin Confidence knew that Wazidul would very soon return to the most common sleeping position, the side position with knees slightly bent.

First, he had to shrink his already tiny body so he was no bigger than a flea and then enter Wazidul's dry mouth. This boy needs to drink more water, Colin Confidence thought! He moved under his tonsils and squirmed his way through the inner workings towards his lower brain. Getting into a brain was always a real struggle as you had to make a big jump and then hang on tightly so you didn't fall backwards into the void around the spinal column.

Colin Confidence made the jump. He did it. He hung on with all his might but must have landed too firmly as Wazidul started to squirm around and then gave a huge cough. Colin Confidence was holding on tighter than he had ever done before; his small hands were holding on to the soft flesh as he was being shaken all about.

Phew, he thought. Suddenly he was moving again. Wazidul was turning onto his side which affected where Colin Confidence needed to get to.

Once Wazidul was still again, Colin Confidence needed to get his bearings as he didn't want to head into the wrong part of his brain area. He lifted his hand and licked it. He then held it up to see which direction the breath was coming in. Lungs were south so he needed to go north. He turned his finger around to detect the warm breath on his dampened digit. He was east so needed to head left.

Colin Confidence needed to get a move on, this was taking longer than he had thought. To save time, he pulled out the mesh he needed from his bag. This needed to cover Wazidul's thought zone so that only good thoughts about Nazim got through and the mean ones would get stuck to the netting. Colin Confidence would take the mean thoughts away with him when he removed the filter later. He headed quickly out of Wazidul's mind.

Part two was now complete, although Colin Confidence did lose his direction a little and nearly ended up leaving through Wazidul's tear duct, which never did Blink fluff any good due to its saltiness.

Colin Confidence looked at his watch. It was 3.47am. Time was tight but it was possible. Next was to visit Mum. She had impressed Colin Confidence a lot but was still making several errors that could be quickly resolved.

He wasted no time and headed in through her left nostril and straight towards the practical ideas area. He had been worried that time may be short here so he had written down a list of little things that Mum could do to help Nazim in a big way.

The list read:

- o Ask Nazim questions that need fuller answers rather than *yes* or *no*

- o Meeting up with Ellis will be scary – talk with him before he goes to help him prepare

- o Let Nazim answer rather than answering for him – he has a voice

- o Be super enthusiastic when he makes positive choices

- o Make sure you always look him in the eye when you talk to him as this develops trust and will help him do it with others

The list was gently secured to Mum's brain zone and slowly dissolved to absorb the information as it went. Getting out was always such a relief, as getting stuck was a tale that many a Blink could tell you about!

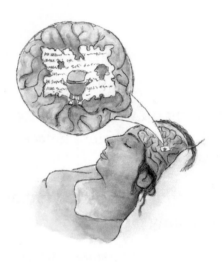

Three down, one to go. Now for Dad. This was the hardest of the night. If anyone could get it wrong with a shy child, it was Dad. Colin Confidence had spent a lot of time that day thinking about how he could have the biggest impact on Dad. A trip down memory lane was the idea that won out.

As you can imagine, tinkering with people's dreams takes some doing. This was where the special spanner came in very handy. The cogs that influence dreams are in many parts of the brain. Colin Confidence was most interested in the memory cogs. This would most likely involve gentle tweaks to nudge Dad into seeing Nazim's shyness in a different way and more importantly, begin changing his own behaviour.

Colin Confidence went in for the final time that night. The long-term memory cogs sit at the back of the lower part of the brain and the tiny Blink headed straight there, spanner in hand.

In just over 10 minutes, Colin Confidence arrived where he needed to be and made several turns to some very large brain cogs. Some of Dad's distant memories flashed up like they were being played on a cinema screen and so Colin Confidence knew he just needed to wait for a sad memory from Dad's childhood. It didn't take very long at all before the perfect image showed up in the memory bank.

Colin Confidence turned the spanner with all his might to lock the memory in. This would then travel around the dream circuit and give Dad a dream he wouldn't forget in a long while but which would help him to support Nazim rather than push him away. He looked at his watch. It was 5.05am, pretty perfect as Dad got up at 6am and so this memory would be the freshest in his mind as he awoke.

Colin Confidence quickly headed out for some fresh air and to let his body finally expand to its normal size again. He needed to hang around as he wanted to see if there were any differences after his hard night's work.

He decided to perch on top of the lampshade on the landing. All the bedrooms led off from that area and so he would have the best view of any developments as they occurred. He was also hopeful of having a very long and slow stretch. Tonight, he had had an extreme Blinks' workout and his body was feeling it. Up there he could restore it without anyone hearing the creaking of his inflating body!

Chapter 15

Where's my family gone?

Slowly but surely, the Alam household rose just like the morning sun. The staggered alarms beeped at different time intervals around the house. Dad's went off first at 6.00am and once he was out of the bathroom, that was the cue for Mum to begin her morning routine. As Mrs Alam finished, she popped her head around Rukkiah's door so that she too could begin her morning preparations. Next was Wazidul and finally Nazim.

In the master bedroom. Dad seemed quieter than usual. "Are you okay?" asked Mum.

"Yes," replied Dad slowly. "I had the most vivid dream last night which has left me feeling quite emotional."

"What was it?"

"I was about Nazim's age and my shyness all came back to me. I felt every one of those difficult feelings again. Feelings I have tried so hard to bury. I was flooded with nervousness, fear, anxiety, loneliness and frustration. It felt awful and some of those feelings are still here with me now."

Mrs Alam stroked Dad on his back in a reassuring way.

"A horrible part of the dream though was that no-one was there for me at all. Whenever anyone came into the dream they turned their back on me or shouted at me. There was no-one to go to, no-one to help, no-one to say it could get better. The worse part was that everything I dreamt was true, it all happened. It wasn't just a dream it was real, it was a real memory."

"Maybe this is a good thing. Nazim

needs you now more than ever before and he needs you to understand."

"I haven't been very understanding, have I?" I was more focussed on pushing him towards the result rather than supporting him through it. Well no more. I have let him down. I've been far too impatient, pushy and rejecting of who my son is. Today that will all change."

Mum smiled, feeling that this could be only a good thing. At the same time, she too was reminded of a few things that had come to her in the night and how she was going to make sure that meeting up with Ellis was a positive thing. She was going to nudge Nazim to talk more rather than try to protect him from what he found difficult.

Wazidul popped his head into his parents' bedroom. "Have I been really awful to Nazim lately?"

Dad looked round in surprise. "I think we all have, son. It's only your mum who has supported Nazim lately. I had my eyes opened in a dream last night. All the negative things we say to him must stop if we want this to get any better. Agreed?" asked Dad.

Wazidul nodded, struggling to think of any of the negative things he might have even said about his lovely and gentle younger brother.

Suddenly Rukkiah rushed into the bedroom.

"I can hear this constant sound in my ear Mum, it sounds like a radio is on but really low. I can't make out what it is saying but it is there all the time. Will you have a look inside?"

Colin Confidence sat up with a jolt! Being so busy with his night time jobs and the morning approaching quicker than he expected, he had forgotten to remove the thought machine from inside Rukkiah's inner ear! What was he going to do? He needed it back as it was a very special piece of Blinks' kit.

He tiptoed into Mum and Dad's bedroom where Mum was peering inside Rukkiah's ear. "I can't see anything." She took a piece of toilet paper and rolled it into a cone so she could clean or remove anything that might be there.

"Oh, there is a tiny bit of black there, let me see if I can get it." Mum gently turned the tissue and extracted the small black speck. They both looked at it and presumed it was some dirt.

"It's gone Mum, thanks so much. What can it have been? That was awful."

"I have no idea but it is sorted now so that is a good thing. Maybe it was some wax that had got lodged."

From behind a bottle of moisturiser, Colin Confidence could see Mum move across to the toilet where she was about to flush the tissue away. He couldn't let this happen but what could he do in five seconds to stop this? He pushed the jar of face cream with all his might and sent it crashing into the sink. Mum jumped with a start and the tissue fell to the floor within millimetres of the toilet. Her attention had been changed and the tissue was sitting between the toilet brush and some cleaning liquid.

Colin Confidence quickly removed the thought machine and placed it carefully into his bag. Phew, mission completed successfully. He headed back to the landing. So far, he was pleased with how his evening activity had done what he needed it to do.

Nazim was lying in his bed, moving from sleep to wakefulness. It seemed like a normal day. Everything looked the same, but some things were very much different. Dad had been in already that morning, kissed him on the head and apologised for being unsupportive. Wazidul hadn't shouted his usual morning abuse and Rukkiah hadn't been heard whinging about Nazim being allowed to sleep in longer than everyone else.

Mum popped her head round the door like she usually did. Today she made an extra special effort to look at him fully rather than avoid the eye contact which she knew he struggled with.

"Morning Nazim, what a gorgeous day. You are going to have a great day, I can feel it. Tell me three things that could make today brilliant?"

The positive enthusiasm from Mum

activated Nazim more than ever before.

"I've got PE and we are doing apparatus which I love," said Nazim excitedly, his eyes flitting occasionally onto Mum's loving face.

"Great, what else?"

"Erm, Dad and Wazidul haven't had a go at me yet this morning."

"Double great," said Mum with a residue of sadness about the reality of how these things had affected him.

"And?"

"I have a new friend in Ellis and that makes me feel like I am not alone or so weird anymore."

Mum gave Nazim a huge hug.

"You are talking to us too. That makes me so proud of you and if you can do that with me, you can do it with anyone."

"I can try," said Nazim, although he knew that was easier said than done!

"Come on, let's have breakfast."

As the Alams sat around the kitchen table, the mood was positive. Nazim didn't have eye contact with anyone in case he saw something in their eyes that would destroy the positive feelings he was having about them all. He did answer them when they asked him questions, which was huge progress on his part. Wilf sat by Nazim's feet as usual but that morning Nazim gave him the attention he deserved. He stroked Wilf's soft ears to show him he was as loyal as the puppy was to him.

"You're alright you, Nazim," began Rukkiah. "You used to get on my nerves, being the youngest and cutest. Now I see that I need to enjoy that rather than hate it. You are my little brother and I am going to enjoy you as much as I can before you turn into a grumpy teenager like Wazidul."

"Shut it, Rukkiah," ranted Wazidul. "At least he isn't as annoying as you. You look good today Nazim, nice t-shirt."

Nazim flicked his eyes in the direction of his brother and sister. This was weird, but the strangest was still to come.

"Shhh, you two. Let's not have any negative thoughts towards each other. We are a family and we need to work together, not against each other. Rukkiah, you are loud and moody and beautiful and thoughtful and we love you regardless! Wazidul, you are lazy and grumpy and clever and kind and we love you because of all those things! Nazim, you are gentle and quiet and loving and forgiving and we love you for who you are. You are all fabulous human beings, different in some many ways but all equal loved and special. You all make us very, very proud," said Dad with a lump in his throat.

"I accept each of you for who you are and my biggest wish for you all is for you to be happy."

"Can I please have £50 for some new trainers then?" asked Rukkiah with a cheeky smile on her face.

"Don't push it," said Dad and they all burst out laughing.

Nazim felt a warm glow inside. For the first time, he felt like his family understood him for the person he was and if they could like him even with his shyness, then there was hope for others too. Maybe Ellis was just the start.

The feeling he liked the most was that he now thought that no matter what went on out there in the big world, he had an army of support at home and was no longer alone. This made him feel stronger, like he could maybe cope with things much better than ever before. That felt like the best feeling ever, but how could he keep hold of these feelings and what if they disappeared when Colin Confidence was no longer around?

Chapter 16

Growth

In the weeks and months that followed, Nazim rode the rollercoaster of moving forward and growing into a happier person. Colin Confidence continued to help him understand his shyness and more importantly, the little things that he could do to help him in big ways. Although there were many ups, he did experience more downs than he hoped for.

On the upside, Nazim's relationship with his dad moved from strength to strength. No longer did he feel that he was letting his dad down all the time or that he was a failure. He knew his dad wanted the best for him but gentle nudging got the better results in the end and that made them both happier.

The shyness was always there under the surface. It was a huge part of who Nazim was but it was no longer the huge black cloak that he chose to hide under whenever he could. Eye contact with others improved, although looking at the gap between people's eyes made that a bit easier and no-one seemed to notice the difference. As his confidence grew with people, the more his eyes could brave a glance into their gaze.

Wilf helped Nazim move things forward no end. As he was such a cute and adorable puppy, people still stopped and wanted to fuss him. Nazim developed a script to ease the difficulty of worrying what to say. Most people asked three questions and *usually* in the same order:

1. How old is he?

2. What breed of dog is he?

3. What is he called?

As you may have noticed I said *usually* in the same order, so usually it all went to plan. Nazim was really tested one day when took Wilf out for a walk in the park. It was all going so well until four dogs bounded over to fuss Wilf! Nazim and Wilf both looked surprised and a bit frightened. Wilf rolled over terrified and did a wee out of fear; Nazim's brain went to mush in the awkwardness that followed. The lovely old lady couldn't apologise enough but left thinking Wilf was called Beagle Cross, which she found a bit odd!

Other ups were the fact that Nazim's brain didn't spend forever over-thinking negative situations anymore. The incident in the park with the old lady would have stopped him taking Wilf out again for weeks. Instead, he challenged what he thought the old lady could be thinking of him and that made it feel better much quicker. He also became kinder on himself and ended up laughing at situations (Wilf doing a scared wee!) rather than taking them too seriously.

School also became an easier place to be. Mrs Waters got a group of lovely children together who all needed a gentle push towards making new friends and they all met in the library at breaks and lunchtimes. One of the girls in the group, Morna, took Nazim's mind out of his shyness many times. She once told him that she felt empty of love a lot, like she couldn't read the language of love. This made Nazim work harder to try and be her friend and slowly it began to happen.

Nazim also developed a great friendship with Ellis. Mum had been brilliant in helping him prepare for their first meet up and thinking about how it might go, before it was thrust upon him. This going well added another layer to their ever-growing bond.

These situations all helped Nazim to develop newer, more positive beliefs about who he was and what people might be thinking of him. They also helped him take his time with situations and not throw himself in at the deep end, something he usually did and which most often made any situation worse. Spending time with friends and being a friend to himself made Nazim feel more in control and helped him think more realistic thoughts about situations. He started to become generally calmer and less fearful of everything. Sadly, not every day produced such delicious experiences.

The down days were hard, possibly even harder than when he used to have them every day. Having tasted the alternative, the bitterness of a difficult day really stung.

He still found breaking old habits hard to do, like when some of the kids in his year made sly comments about him being so quiet. It still hurt and he often wondered how many hours or days he had spent listening to negative thoughts before he realised he was doing it.

He also wasn't sure he would ever shake off the self-conscious feelings he had when he was around people and the thoughts *he* implanted into *their* heads about *him* still challenged his thinking most days. It was on these days that Colin Confidence was always the most welcomed.

Nevertheless, Nazim made huge progress and Colin Confidence came to visit one last time.

"So Nazim, haven't you done brilliantly? When I think back to the young person I met all of those months ago, it is so wonderful to see how you have developed."

"It's all thanks to you, Colin Confidence. I couldn't have done it without you," replied Nazim gratefully.

"It's all thanks to you, Nazim. I can only make suggestions, you decide whether you are going to do it or not. You have worked so hard. You made the improvements, you did the work," smiled Colin Confidence. "You have the tools now, it is up to you to use them."

"What about on difficult days? That is when I need you the most," said Nazim anxiously.

"Over the last few months, I have visited you less and less on those days so that you learned to do this yourself. Don't forget that doing it yourself doesn't mean doing it alone. It means using the support you have around you.

Remember last week when school was tough and you felt that you were back to square one? You went to your dad and talked to him about how you felt. That is one of the Blink rules, you must share your difficulties with the adults who care about you and you do that so naturally now. That is why I feel I can move on now to help a different child. You have passed with flying colours, Nazim. You are a star!"

Nazim smiled but couldn't hide his sadness at the thought of losing his special buddy.

"You will be okay. I wouldn't be leaving you if I didn't think you were ready. This is the hardest part for both of us. Ending a project makes me really happy because it means you have succeeded, but really sad too because I will miss you," explained Colin Confidence.

"Yes, I know. I couldn't be happier with how things have gone, even though I know there will be more challenges ahead. I will miss you so much. You believed in me and helped me believe in myself. Even my family have changed the way they think of me." Nazim looked at Colin Confidence with curiosity. "Did you do that as well?"

Colin Confidence tightened his lips and looked up to the sky in an 'I'm not telling' sort of way.

They both started laughing.

"Can I ask you one last question before you go?" asked Nazim.

"Fire away."

"What if all these good feelings disappear and I go back to the old me?"

"There is no old you Nazim, just old ways. You are still you and always will be. You are gentle, quiet and sensitive. The difference is that your brain is different now due to the way you see these qualities. You have grown and your brain has grown with you. You might feel similar feelings occasionally but you are a different Nazim. Just keep up the good work and it will all be good."

"But what if I forget it all. Will I go backwards again?"

"The problems you had before were because your higher brain wasn't in charge. You had become a slave to your shyness. Your brain is skilled for life now and the longer you practise, the easier it will become.

Colin Confidence pulled out a folded piece of paper. "Let's recap some of the most important points to keep you challenging your shyness:

- ✓ Accept and love yourself for who you are rather than resist your negative traits

- ✓ Challenge negative thoughts about who you are

- ✓ Stop yourself planting your thoughts into to other peoples' heads, you are not a mind reader!

- ✓ When something feels difficult, do little things and see what happens. Think of them as mini experiments

- ✓ What is the worst that could happen? If you prepare for the worst then whatever happens is usually better

- ✓ Reduce the amount of time you let yourself focus on negative thinking – re-focus on positive thinking

- ✓ Act like you want to feel

✓ When your shyness feels strong, focus on what is happening on the outside of you rather than what is happening on the inside of you

✓ When you feel a success, do the same thing again soon after to keep building your confidence

✓ Be realistic – you are awesome!

Colin Confidence handed the paper to Nazim. "Remember these key rules to overcome shyness and you won't go wrong."

Nazim slipped the piece of paper into his bedside cabinet drawer. "I will read them regularly, I promise."

"Then I'm confident you will be okay! Goodbye, Nazim. Stay wonderful." They shook hands and on the final shake, Colin Confidence had disappeared and was on his way to his week of wonderfulness.

Nazim looked around his room and caught a glimpse of himself in the wardrobe mirror. He sat taller with his shoulders arched backwards and although he didn't truly feel it, he definitely looked more confident. Maybe the words of Colin Confidence were right after all, his name certainly rang true. Fake it till you make it. Well he was definitely going to continue giving it a go.

Why don't you? What have you got to lose?!

Acknowledgements

This book, as with all the others in this series, has a core team of wonderful people who transport it from the words that leave my brain into the book you are reading now! Firstly, thank you so much to Auntie Karin, Lily, Amanda, Jill and Janet, who help me to simplify my geeky psychology brain and focus on the basics when I am immersed in the land of The Blinks' magic. Your awesomeness means more to me than you could ever know.

As always, Rachel Pesterfield has managed to bring this book to life with her fabulous illustrations and commitment to detail. Rachel, you really are a star and never forget that. Thanks also to Gail who is constantly supportive and positive towards the core principles of my books.

Also to Vanessa, my dedicated PA, who has enhanced my working life no end!

A massive thank you also goes to Hallam FM's Cash 4 Kids who, for the second year running, is sponsoring 'The Blinks' books and providing copies to as many primary schools as possible in the South Yorkshire area.

I would also like to say a huge thank you to my ever-supportive family and my wonderful friends for always believing in me and being there whenever I feel a bit zapped!

Finally, it is always important to me to recognise the wonderful people who have moved on from our lives this year and may well just feed into the creation of future Blinks. Some are people I know personally, some are special to those I care about and some are creative legends. Please share a moment to remember Arthur, Bob, Michael, Terry, Bruce Forsyth and Glen Campbell.

About The Author

Andrea Chatten - MSc, MBPsS,
PGCL&M, BEd(Hons), Dip.CBT

Andrea Chatten has been a specialised

teacher for over 25
years, working with
children from ages
5-16 with emotional
and behavioural
difficulties. She is
currently working
as 'Lead Children's
Emotional & Behavioural Psychologist' at
Unravel CEBPC with schools and families
in Sheffield.

Developing positive, trusting
relationships has always been at the
heart of her practice with children and
young people in order to nudge them

into improved psychological well-being. Over the years, Andrea has developed and applied many positive developmental psychology approaches.

This insight is incorporated into her stories in order to help children, young people and their families to gain more of an understanding and potential strategies to try, in order to deal with a range of behavioural issues that children and young people could experience.

Andrea created 'The Blinks' so that parents could also benefit from reading the books with their children, particularly if they identify with the children in the stories and their family circumstances.

Both parent and child can learn how to manage early forms of psychological distress as a natural part of growing up rather than it become problematic when not addressed in its early stages.

The Blinks' is a series of books that discreetly apply lots of psychological theory throughout the story including Cognitive Behavioural Therapy, Developmental and Positive Psychology approaches.

This book in the series tackles the issue of shyness and how to prevent this everyday cognition from becoming more serious anxiety in the future.

www.unravelcebpc.co.uk

Facebook - /Theblinksbooks
Twitter - @BlinksThe

THE BLINKS REFERENCE MANUALS

Accompanying each of 'The Blinks' novels is a Reference Manual for parents, carers, older siblings, teachers, and professionals.

The supporting manual for each novel provides a greater understanding of the psychology of each title; worry, anger, self-esteem, and sadness (other titles are being created) and how it can impact on emotional developmental and well-being.

It also provides lots of 'top tips' on what works best for children and young people whilst growing up and some activity questions that can be used as a starting point to initiate emotive dialogue or discussion.

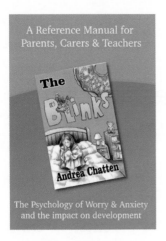

The Blinks

"Worry"

Reference Manual

The Blinks

"Anger"

Reference Manual

The Blinks

"Self-Esteem"

Reference Manual

The Blinks

"Sad"

Reference Manual

OTHER TITLES IN THE BLINKS
SERIES OF NOVELS

The Blinks - Worry

When Amanda is discussed at the midnight meeting, she is lucky to become part of some very special Blink intervention. As a result, Amanda begins to make changes she never thought possible.

The Blinks - Anger

Robbie's life has never been great, but the events over the last few years have slowly made him more and more unhappy and angry. One day it all gets too much, and his anger erupts! Through a series of events, Robbie learns just who is responsible for his anger and how to deal with it.

The Blinks - Self-Esteem

Bladen and Tim are twins who have spent many years being unkind to each other. This has not helped them to develop very positive feelings. Their low self-esteem has affected their confidence, friendships, and their happiness. Larry Love-Who-You-Are recognises works hard to help the twins overcome some very personal challenges.

The Blinks - Sad

Shan is a normal girl who has a normal life in many way, but one thing Shan has which many other children don't have is buckets and buckets of sadness. Thankfully, Marlowe Mindful sees Shan as someone who is ready for Blinks' support and begins the process of helping her understand her sadness and how to change her feelings for the better.

IN ORDER TO PURCHASE ANY OF THE BLINKS
NOVELS OR MANUALS PLEASE GO TO:
www.theblinks.co.uk